They were on a great veldt, where endless herds of game grazed and vultures circled overhead. Luke and Mrs. Withers stood by the Aperture to mark it while Roger walked away through the sea of chest-high grass.

Fifteen minutes later, he approached the same spot from behind.

"Still trapped," Roger said. "Let's go on."

They passed . . . through . . . and the daylight winked out—

—to be replaced by an all-enclosing gray. For an instant, Roger teetered on one toe, struggling for balance. Then a giant hand closed on his body, yanked him up, around, and out into the brilliant light of a vast, white-floored room.

TIME TRAP

KEITH LAUMER

TIME TRAP

BAEN BOOKS

TIME TRAP

Copyright © 1970 by Keith Laumer

A Baen Book

Baen Publishing Enterprises
260 Fifth Avenue
New York, N.Y. 10001

First Baen printing, July 1987

ISBN: 0-671-65340-7

Cover art by Erin McKee

Printed in the United States of America

Distributed by
SIMON & SCHUSTER
1230 Avenue of the Americas
New York, N.Y. 10020

PROLOGUE

1

Machinist's Mate Second Class Joe Acosta, on duty in the deckhouse of the Coast Guard cutter *Hampton*, squinted across the dazzling waters of Tampa Bay at the ungainly vessel wallowing in the light sea half a mile off the port bow.

"What the heck is that, skipper?" He addressed the lieutenant standing beside him with binoculars trained on the spectacle.

"Two-master; odd-looking high stern. Sails hanging in rags. Looks like she's been in a stiff blow," the officer said. "Let's take a closer look."

The cutter changed course, swinging in a wide arc to approach the square-rigged vessel. At close range, Acosta saw the weathered timbers of the clumsy hull, where scraps of scarlet paint and gilt still clung. Clustered barnacles and trailing seaweed marked the waterline. The power boat passed under the ship's stern at a distance of fifty feet; ornate letters almost obliterated by weathering spelled out the name *Cucaracha*.

As the boat throttled back, a wrinkled brown face appeared at the rail above; worried coal-black eyes looked into Acosta's. Other men appeared beside the first, clad in rags, uniformly pockmarked, gap-toothed, and unshaven.

"Skipper, this must be a load of them Cuban refugees!" Acosta hazarded. "But how'd they get this far without being spotted?"

The officer shook his head. "They must be making a movie," he said. "This can't be for real."

"You ever seen a tub like that before?" Acosta inquired.

"Only in the history books."

"I see what you mean. It's kind of like the *Bounty* they got anchored over at the pier at St. Pete."

"Something like that. Only this is a galleon, late sixteenth-century type. Portuguese, from the flag."

"Looks like somebody could have told us about it," Acosta said. "Hey, you on deck!" He cupped his hands and shouted to the faces above. "If that tub draws more than two fathoms, you got problems!" He jerked a thumb over his shoulder. "Shoal waters!" he added.

The man who had first appeared called out something in a hoarse voice.

"Hey," Acosta said. "I was right. He's talking some kind o' Spanish." He cupped his hands again.

"*¿Quién son ustedes? ¿Qué pasa?*" The man on deck shouted at some length, making the sign of the cross as he did.

"What did he say?" the officer inquired.

Acosta shook his head. "He talks funny, skipper. He must think we're part of the movie."

"We'll go aboard and take a look."

An hour later, a line aboard the derelict, the cutter headed for the Port Tampa quarantine wharf.

"What do you think?" Joe Acosta asked, eyeing the skipper sidelong.

"I think we've got a galleon crewed by thirteen illiterate Portuguese in tow," the officer snapped. "Outside of that, I'm not thinking."

2

At 10:15 A.M., as was her unalterable custom, Mrs. L. B. (Chuck) Withers put on her hat, checked her hemline in the front-hall mirror, and set out on the ten-minute walk into town. She passed the long-defunct service station at the bend, walking briskly, head up, back straight, breathed in for four paces, out for four, a simple routine to which she ascribed full credit for the remarkable youthfulness of her thirty-six-year-old figure.

A minute or two after passing the station, Mrs. Withers slowed, sensing some indefinable strangeness in the aspect of the road ahead. She had long ago ceased to notice her surroundings on her walks, but now an unfamiliar sign caught her eye ahead:

BRANTVILLE—1 MILE

It was curious, she thought, that they should bother to erect a new sign here—especially an erroneous one. Her house was precisely one half-mile from town; it couldn't be more than a few hundred yards from here to the city limits. Closer, she saw that the sign was not new; the paint was

chalky and faded, peppered by a passing marks-
man with a pair of rust-edged pits. She looked
around uneasily; now that she noticed, this stretch
didn't look precisely familiar, somehow. There—
that big sweetgum tree with the 666 sign—surely
she would have noticed that. . . .

She hurried on, eager for a cheery glimpse of
the Coca-Cola billboard around the gentle curve of
the road. Instead she saw a white-painted building, patchily visible through the foliage. The brick
chimney had a curiously familiar look. She pressed
on, passed the shelter of the line of tall poplars—
and halted, staring indignantly at her own house.
She had left it, walking east—and now she was
approaching it from the west. It was preposterous—
impossible!

Mrs. Withers settled her hat firmly on her head.
Very well: daydreaming, she had taken some turn
(not that she had ever seen any branching road
between home and town) that had brought her in
a circle back to her own door. It was a nonsensical
mistake, and the widow of L. B. Withers had no
patience with nonsense, which was best dealt with
by ignoring it. Grasping her handbag in both hands
as one would a set of reins, she marched determinedly past the front gate.

Five minutes later, with a mounting apprehen-
sion stirring beneath her ribs, she approached a
sign planted by the roadside:

BRANTVILLE—1 MILE

For a moment she stared at the letters; then she
whirled and marched back the way she had come.

At her gate, she caught at the post, breathing hard, collecting herself. The sight of the familiar front porch with the broken lattice that Mr. Withers had always been going to fix but somehow never had gotten around to calmed her. She took a deep breath and forced her respiration back to normal. She had almost made a fool of herself, running into the house and telephoning the sheriff with an hysterical tale of mixed-up roads. Hmmph! Interesting gossip *that* would make in town, with half of the old lechers there already smirking lewdly at her as they made their sly remarks about women who lived alone. Very well, she'd gotten confused, twice taken a wrong turning, even if she hadn't noticed any place where a body could *take* a wrong turning. This time she'd watch every step of the way, and if she arrived at the post office half an hour later than usual, she dared anybody to make a remark about it!

This time when the sign appeared ahead, she halted in the middle of the road, looking both ways, torn between a desire to run ahead and catch a glimpse of the town's edge and an equal desire to flee back to the familiarity of the house.

"It can't be," she said aloud, and was shocked at the undisciplined break in her voice. "I've walked along this road a thousand times! There's no way to get lost. . . ."

The sound of the word "lost," with its implication of incompetence, had the effect of rousing a renewed surge of healthy indignation. Lost indeed! A sober, God-fearing, respectable adult woman didn't get lost in broad daylight, like some drunken hobo! If she was confused, it was because the road had been changed! And now that she thought of it, that was no doubt the explanation: during the night, the road people had brought in their equipment and cut a new road through— everybody knew how quickly they could do it these days—without even telling anyone. The idea! And the new sign fitted in with it. Her jaw set determinedly, Mrs. Withers turned and started for home with a firm tread. This time she'd call the sheriff, and give that self-satisfied old fool a piece of her mind.

The busy signal went on and on. After dialing five times, Odelia Withers went into the kitchen, rigidly holding her expression of righteous disapproval, opened the icebox door, and began mechanically setting out lunch. Fortunately there was food on hand; it wasn't that she *had* to shop today. Carefully holding her thoughts from her aborted walk to town, she prepared a sandwich from the last of the boiled ham and poured a glass of milk, seated herself in a ray of sunlight streaming past the ruffled curtains, and ate, listening to the tick of the clock in the hall.

She tried the telephone ten times in all during the afternoon. First the sheriff's office, then the Highway Patrol, then the city police. The lines were all busy; probably a flood of complaints about the road. Then, on impulse, she dialed Henry, the mechanic at the station in town. Another busy signal. She tried the numbers of two of her friends, then the operator. All busy.

She tuned the radio to her favorite program, a harrowing drama of small-town PTA politics, and busied herself cleaning the already spotless house until the shadows of late afternoon lay across the lawn. After dinner she tried one more call, hung up as the instrument emitted its impersonal *zawwp, zawwp, zawwp* . . .

The next morning she walked as far as the sign before returning home, filled with frustrating desire to complain to someone. Without thinking, she went to the icebox, took out the ham and the milk.

She frowned at the meat on the plate. Three slices. But she had eaten the last of the ham yesterday, two slices for lunch, the other in a salad at dinnertime. And the milk: she had finished it, put the empty bottle by the door. . . .

She went to the cupboard, took down the jar of mayonnaise she had opened yesterday, removed the lid. The jar was full, untouched.

Odelia Withers proceeded to prepare lunch, eat, and wash the dishes. Then she put on a sun hat and went into the garden to cut flowers, an expression of determined disapproval on her face.

3

"It's a kook item," Bill Summers, the "Personalities" editor of *Scene* magazine, said in his usual tone of weary disparagement. "But that doesn't mean it's not news."

"Some guy goes poking around in the off-limits section of an Arab town and gets a mob after him," Bud Vetch, *Scene*'s number one field man, said. "Maybe that's a hot item to the local U. S. Embassy, but what's it to the public?"

"Didn't you look at the pics?"

Vetch yawned as Summers passed the three five-by-eight glossies across to him. "So some tourist had a Brownie with him," he said. "Amateur photo hounds . . ." His voice faded as he looked at the top picture. It showed a tall, ungainly, stoop-shouldered man with a hollow face, deep-set eyes, a short black beard, a prominent wart, dressed in a dowdy black suit and a high hat. In the background were visible a crowd of white-robed men around a merchant's stall. Vetch looked at the next shot. It showed the man seated at a table under an awning, bushy head bared, fanning himself with the hat, apparently deep in conversation with a khaki-uniformed native policeman. The third photo was a close-up of the lined face, looking back, with a slightly surprised expression.

"Hey!" Vetch said. "This looks like—"

"Yes," Summers cut him off. "I know all the wise remarks you're going to make. I don't know what this bird's angle is, but if he wanted to attract attention, he did it with bells on. The locals don't have a very good idea of chronology. An official inquiry came through to Washington this morning from their Foreign Office, and State had to send them a formal reply, confirming the man in question was dead. That's when the chili really hit the fan. The Tamboolans say they've seen pictures and they have a positive ID on this character, and that he's very much alive. Either that, or he's an afreet. Either way, it's a problem. I want you to get there before the bubble bursts and interview this fellow."

Vetch was still studying the photos. "It's uncanny," he said. "If this is makeup or a mask, it's a top-quality job."

"What do you mean, 'if'?"

"Nothing—I guess," Vetch said. "By the way, did this fellow give a name?"

"Sure," Summers grunted. "He told them he was Abraham Lincoln."

4

"I'm glad to see the last of that sin-killer," Job Arkwright growled, standing at the cabin door, watching the slight, dandified figure in the incongruously elegant greatcoat and boots disappear along the snow-blanketed path into the deep shadows of the virgin forest.

"It were a mean trick, Mr. Arkwright, making poor Fly help you cut all that cordwood—and then sending the poor slicker out in this weather," Charity Arkwright said. "After all, he's a preacher—even if he does have that sweet little mustache."

"I'll sweeten his mustache!" Arkwright glowered at his mate, a young, large-eyed woman with an ample bosom and slim waist. "If you'd of went ahead and fattened up like I ast you, you wouldn't have no trouble with them kind of fellers!"

"No trouble," Charity murmured, and patted her hair. "All the while you were out hunting rabbits, he set by the fire and read scripture to me. My, didn't I learn a lot!"

"Well—just so he didn't get no idears."

"Fiddle-dee-dee! I didn't give him a chance to."

"I wisht I knew jist how to take that," Job muttered. "Looky here, girl, did he—"

"Hark! What's that?" Charity cupped a hand to her ear. "Somebody coming?"

Job grabbed his muzzle-loader down from its place and swung the door open. "Can't be no hostiles," he said. "They don't make that kind o' racket!" He stepped outside. "You stay here," he ordered. "I'll have a look-see."

He moved to the corner of the cabin. The crashing sounds from the underbrush approached steadily from the deep woods to the rear of the house. The brush parted and a bedraggled figure emerged from the last entangling thicket and halted, staring across toward the cabin.

"Who's that?" Job barked.

"Why—'tis I, Fly Fornication Beebody," a breathless voice came back. "Brother Arkwright—is it thee, in sooth?"

"Who else? Ain't nobody else in these parts. How'd you get around back? And what the devil are ye doing there? I thought you was headed for Jerubabbel Knox's farm when you left here."

"Don't take the name of the Fiend lightly," Fly gasped, coming up, his round face glowing with sweat in spite of the bitter cold. "I warrant, Brother Arkwright, I see his foul hand in this! I struck due east for Knox's stead, and the treacherous path led me back to thy door."

"Fly, you got a bottle hid?" Job demanded. He leaned toward the itinerant parson and sniffed sharply.

"Would I play thee false in that fashion?" Beebody retorted. "What I'd not warrant for a goodly sup of honest rum at this moment!"

"Come on; I'll set ye on the trail," Job said. He went into the cabin for his coat, then led at a brisk

pace with Beebody panting at his heels. The trail
wound around a giant pine tree, skirted a boulder,
angled upward across a rise. Arkwright paused,
frowning about him, then went on. The trail
dwindled, vanished in a tangle of dead berry
vines.

"Arkwright—we're lost!" Fly Beebody gasped.
"Beelzebub has set a snare for us—"

"Have done, ye fool!" Arkwright snapped. "The
path's overgrowed, that's all!" He forced his way
through the dense growth. Ahead, the trees seemed
to thin. He made for the clearing, stepped into the
open—

There was a deafening *boom!* and a heavy slug
whickered through the icy branches by Job's ear.
He threw himself flat, gaping in amazement at the
cabin, the corn shed, the frozen garden patch, the
woman with the muzzle-loader in her hands.

"Charity!" he yelled. "It's me!"

Half an hour later, in the cabin, Fly Beebody
was still shaking his head darkly.

"I'll make my couch in the snow if need be," he
said. "But I'll not set foot i' that bewitched forest
'ere tomorrow's dawn."

"You can lie here, i' the shed," Job said grudg-
ingly. "If you must." Charity offered the involun-
tary guest a quilt, which he accepted with ill
grace. He departed, grumbling, and Job barred
the door.

Husband and wife slept poorly that night. Shortly
before dawn, they were awakened by a frantic
pounding on the door. Job leaped up, opened it,
gun in hand. Fly Beebody stood there, disheveled,
coatless. He stuttered, then pointed.

Tall in the misty light of pre-dawn, the mighty cottonwood tree which the two men had with such labor felled the previous day stood once more in its accustomed place, untouched by the axe.

CHAPTER ONE

1

Roger Tyson flipped the windshield wipers into high gear as the spatter of rain became a downpour, then a deluge. He slowed to fifty, his headlight beams soaked up and absorbed by the solid curtains of whirling water sheeting across the blacktop. Lightning winked and thunder banged like artillery.

"Perfect," Tyson congratulated the elements. "What a way to end up: the middle of the night, in the middle of nowhere, with no gas, no money, no credit card." His stomach rumbled. "Not even a ham sandwich. Something tells me I'm not fitted to survive in the harsh modern world."

A broken seat spring prodded him painfully; water trickled down from under the dash and dripped on his knee. The engine gasped three times, backfired, and died.

"Oh, no," he groaned, steering to the side of the road and off onto the shoulder. He turned up his coat collar, climbed out in the driving rain,

13

lifted the hood. The engine looked like an engine. He closed the hood, stood with his hands in his pockets, staring off down the dark road.

"Probably won't be a car along for a week," he reflected dismally. "Only a damned fool would be out in this weather—and not even a damned fool would stop, even if he came along here, and—" His ruminations were interrupted by a glint of light in the distance; the faint sound of an approaching engine cut through the drum of the rain.

"Hey!" Roger brightened. "Someone's coming!" He trotted out into the center of the road, watching the light grow as it rushed toward him. He waved his arms.

"Hey, stop!" he yelled as the oncoming vehicle showed no indication of slowing. "Stop!" He leaped aside at the last instant as a low-slung motorcycle leaped out of the gloom, a slim, girlish figure crouched behind the windshield. He caught just a glimpse of her shocked expression as she swerved to miss him. The speeding bike went into a skid, slid sideways forty feet, and plunged off the road. There was a prolonged crashing and snapping of wood and metal, a final resounding crunch, and silence.

"Good Lord!" Roger skittered across the road, picked his way down the steep bank, following the trail of snapped-off saplings. At the bottom, the crumpled machine lay on its side, one chrome-plated wire wheel turning lazily, the headlight still shining upward through the wet leaves. The girl lay a few feet away, on her back, eyes shut.

Roger squatted at her side, reached for her pulse. Her eyes opened: pale green eyes, gazing into his.

"You must help me," she whispered with obvious effort.

"Sure," Roger gulped. "Anything at all! I—I'm sorry. . . ."

"The message," the girl whispered. "It's of the utmost importance. It must be delivered. . . ."

"Look, I'll have to go back up by my car and try to flag somebody down."

"Don't bother," the girl whispered. "My neck is broken. I have only a few seconds to live. . . ."

"Nonsense," Roger choked. "You'll be right as rain in a few days—"

"Don't interrupt," the girl said sharply. "The message: Beware the Rhox!"

"What rocks?" Roger looked around wildly. "I don't see any rocks!"

"For your sake—I hope you never do," the victim gasped. "The message must be delivered at once! You must go . . ." Her voice faltered. "Too late," she breathed. "No time . . . to explain . . . take . . . button . . . right ear . . ."

"I'm wasting time!" Roger started to rise. "I'll go for a doctor!" He checked as the girl's lips moved.

"Take . . . the button . . . put it in . . . your ear. . . ." The words were almost inaudible, but the green eyes held on Roger's, pleading.

"Seems like a funny time to worry about a hearing aid," Roger gulped, "but . . ." He lifted a lock of wet black hair aside, gingerly grasped the small gold button tucked into the girl's delicately moulded ear. As he withdrew it, the light of awareness faded from the girl's glazing eyes. Roger grabbed for her wrist, felt a final feeble thump-thump of the pulse—then nothing.

"Hey!" Roger stared uncomprehending at the white, perfect-featured face. "You can't be . . . I mean, I didn't . . . you mustn't . . ." He gulped hard, blinking back sudden tears.

"She's dead," he breathed. "And all because of me! If I hadn't jumped out in front of her like that, she'd still be alive!" Badly shaken, he tucked the gold button in his pocket, climbed back up the slope, slipping and sliding. Back in his car, he used tissues to mop off his face and hands.

"What a mess," he groaned. "I ought to be put in jail! I'm a murderer! Not that my being in jail would help any. Not that anything I could do would help any!" He took the button out and examined it under the dash light. There were thin filaments trailing from it, probably leads to a battery in the owner's pocket.

He rolled the bean-sized button between his fingers. "She seemed to think this was important; used her dying breath to tell me about it. Wanted me to stick it in my ear. . . ." He held the tiny object to his ear. Did he hear a faint, wavering hum, or was it his imagination? He pushed it farther in. There was a faint tickling sensation, tiny rustling and popping sounds. He tried to withdraw the button, felt a sharp pain—

"Drive to Pottsville, one hundred and two miles, north-northeast," the dead girl's voice said in his ear. *"Start now. Time is precious!"*

2

There was the sound of an approaching motor. Roger scrambled quickly from the car, peering into the rain, which had settled down now to a steady drizzle. For the second time, a single headlight was approaching along the road.

"Now, this time don't jump out yelling," he cautioned himself. "When they stop, just tell them that you've been driven mad by hardship, and are hearing voices. And don't forget to mention the hallucination about the girl on the motorcycle; that may be an important lead for the psychiatrist." He stood by the side of the car, staring anxiously at the oncoming light, waving his hand in a carefully conservative flagging motion. The vehicle failed to slow; instead, it swung wide, shot past him at full bore—and as it did, he saw the shape behind the handlebars: a headless torso, obese, bulbous, brick-red, pear-shaped, ornamented with two clusters of tentacles, like lengths of flexible metal hose. Through the single goggle, an eye as big as a pizza and similarly pigmented swiveled to impale him with a glance of utter alienness. With a strangled yell, Roger leaped back, tripped, went down hard on the mud-slick pavement. In horror, he saw the motorcycle veer wildly, stand on its nose, hurling its monstrous rider clear, then skid on its side another hundred feet before coming to a stop in the center of the highway.

Roger tottered to his feet and cantered forward, approached the inert form lying motionless on the pavement. From a distance of ten feet, he could see that it would never ride again: the upper portion was smashed into a pulp of the consistency of mashed potatoes.

"Help," Roger said weakly, aware of a loud singing sensation in his ears. In his left ear, to be specific.

"Time is of the essence," the girl's slightly accented voice said. *"Get going!"*

Roger tugged again at the button, was rewarded with another pang.

"I should go to the police," he said. "But what can I say? That I was responsible for the death of a girl and a giant rutabaga?"

"Forget the police," the voice said impatiently. *"I'm maintaining vitality in a small cluster of cortical cells only with the greatest difficulty, in order to hold open this link through the Reinforcer! Don't render the effort useless by dithering here! Start now!"*

"B-but—my car won't start!"

"Take the motorcycle!"

"That would be stealing!"

"Who's going to report it? Relatives of a giant rutabaga?"

"You have a definite point there," Roger said, hurrying toward the fallen machine. "Somehow, I never thought insanity would be like this." He lifted the bike. Except for a few scratches in the green paint, it seemed as good as new. He kicked it into life, mounted, and gunned off down the highway, squinting into the darkness ahead.

3

At the next town, Roger scanned front lawns for a sign indicating the availability of an M.D. "No point in holding out for a high-powered big-city headshrinker," he rationalized. "The old-time small-town GP is the man to see—and he'll be a lot less likely to demand cash in advance."

He spotted what he was looking for, pulled to the curb beside ranked garbage cans in front of a looming, three-story frame house. At once lights went on inside. The door opened, and a small, sharp-nosed man emerged, shading his eyes.

"What'll I tell him?" Roger asked himself, suddenly self-conscious. "I've heard about retarded kids stuffing things up their noses and ears and whatnot, but I'll feel a little foolish explaining how *I* happened to pull a trick like that."

"Who's that?" a scratchy voice called. "Just step inside and lie down on the table. Have you diagnosed in three minutes flat."

"I can't just tell him I stuck it in there cold," Roger reflected. "And if I tell him the real reason . . ."

"No reason to go around worrying about cancer," the sharp-nosed man said, venturing down the brick steps. "Take two minutes and set your mind at rest."

"Suppose he sticks me in a straitjacket and calls for the fellows with the butterfly nets?" the thought occurred to Roger. "They say once you're in, you have a heck of a time getting out again."

"Now, if it's just a touch of TB, I got just the thing." The practitioner was advancing along the walk. "None o' these fancy antibiotics, mind you—cost a fortune. My own patented formula, based on fermented mare's whey. Packs a wallop and good for what ails you!"

"After all, it's not as if it was actually unendurable or anything," Roger pointed out to himself. "Old Uncle Lafcadio carried on for years with a whole troop of little silver men giving him advice from under the wallpaper."

"Tell you what," the healer proposed, producing a bottle from under his coat as he crossed the parched grass strip. "I'll let you have a trial dosage for a dollar twenty-nine including tax; you can't beat them prices this side of K. C."

"Ah . . . no thank you, sir," Roger demurred, revving his engine. "Actually I'm not a patient; I'm a treasury agent on the lookout for excise violations."

"Excuse me, Buster," the little man said. "I just come out to empty the garbage." He lifted the lid of the nearest container and deposited the flat flask therein. Roger felt sharp eyes on him as he let out the clutch and sped off down the street.

"You made the right decision," the small voice said in his ear.

"I'm a coward," Roger groaned. "What do I care what he thinks? Maybe I'd better go back—"

A sharp pang in his ear made him yelp.

"I'm afraid I just can't allow that," his unseen companion stated firmly. *"Just take a left at the next intersection, and we'll be in Pottsville in less than two hours."*

4

One hour and fifty-five minutes later, Roger was wheeling the bike slowly along a garishly lit avenue lined with pawnshops, orange-juice and shoe-shine stands, billiard emporia, and places of refreshment decorated with eight-by-ten glossies of startling candor, all bustling with activity in spite of the hour.

"Slower," the dead girl's voice cautioned. *"Turn in up ahead, that big garage-like place."*

"That's the bus station," Roger said. "If you're planning on my buying a ticket, forget it. I'm broke."

"Nothing like that. We're within a few yards of our objective."

Roger narrowly averted being crushed against the tiled wall by the snorting bulk of an emerging Chicago-bound Greyhound as he steered into the echoing interior. As directed, he abandoned the motorcycle, pushed through the revolving door into the fudgy atmosphere of the waiting room, with its traditional decor of sleeping enlisted personnel and unwed-looking mothers.

"Cross the room," the voice directed. Roger complied, halted on command before a closed door.

"Try in here."

Roger pushed through the door. A corpulent lady with a mouthful of hairpins whirled on him with a shrill cry of alarm. He backed out hastily.

"That was the ladies' room!" he hissed.

"Damn right, Clyde," a bass voice rumbled at his elbow. A large cop eyed him with hostility from a height of at least six-three. "I got my eye on you birds. Dumbrowski runs a clean beat, and don't you forget it!" He bellied closer and lowered his voice. "Uh—by the way: what's it look like in there, anyways?"

"Just like a men's room," Roger gulped. "Practically."

"Yeah? Well, watch yourself, Ralph!"

"Certainly, officer." Roger backed to the adjoining door and stepped inside, urged by the voice. An elderly colored man straightened from his post against the wall.

"Yes, sir," he said briskly. "Shine? Shave? Massage? What about a fast clean and press?"

"No thanks, I just . . ."

"Little something to cut the fog?" He slid a flat bottle from his pocket.

"Say, if you've got TB, you ought to be in Arizona," Roger said.

The Negro gave him a thoughtful look. He removed the cap from the bottle and took a large swallow; he frowned, upended the bottle in the nearest sink.

"Man, you're right," he said. "I can just catch the 2:08 to Phoenix." He left hastily.

"At least I'm not the only one who's insane," Roger muttered.

"The last stall," the girl's voice said. *"Sorry about the mix-up, but I left here in something of a hurry."*

"I should think so!" Roger said. "What were you doing in a men's room?"

"No time to explain now. Just swing that door open."

Roger did so. The cubicle contained the usual plumbing, nothing more.

"A little to the left—there!"

A glowing line had appeared in mid-air, directly over the bowl, shining with a greenish light of its own, brilliant in the gloom. When Roger moved his head a few inches, it disappeared.

"An optical illusion," he said doubtfully.

"By no means. It's an Aperture. Now, here's what I want you to do: write a note—I'll dictate— and simply toss it through. That's all. I'll just have to trust to luck that it lands where I want it to."

"It will land in the local sewage processing plant," Roger protested. "This is the craziest method I ever heard of for delivering mail!"

"*Move a little closer to the Aperture; you'll see it's not as simple as it appears at first glance.*"

Roger edged closer. The line broadened into a ribbon that gleamed with rainbow colors like a film of oil on water. Closer still, it widened to become a shimmering plane that seemed to extend through the walls to infinity. He stepped back, dizzy.

"It was like looking over the edge of the world," he whispered.

"*Close,*" the voice said. "*Now quickly, the note.*"

"I'll have to borrow a pencil." Roger stepped back into the lobby, secured the loan of a gnawed stub from a ticket clerk. Back inside, he took out a crumpled envelope and smoothed it.

"Shoot," he said. "Let's get this over with."

"*Very well, start off 'Dear S'lunt.' Or no, make that 'Technor Second Level S'lunt.' Or maybe 'Dear Technor' would be better. . . .*"

"I don't know how to spell 'Technor,' " Roger said. "And I'm not sure about 'S'lunt.' "

"*It doesn't matter. Let's just launch right into the matter: 'My attempt to traverse Axial Channel partially successful. Apparent Museum and associated retrieval system work of advanced race capable of manipulations in at least two superior orders of dimensionalty. Recommend effort to dispatch null-engine to terminal coordinates to break temporal stasis. Signed, Q'nell, Field Agent.'*"

"What does all that mean?" Roger queried.

"*Never mind! Did you get it all down?*"

"I missed the part after 'My attempt.' "

The voice repeated the message. Roger copied it out in block capitals.

"Now pitch it through the Aperture, and you're finished," the voice said.

As Roger made a move to step into the stall, two men burst through the outer door. One was the ticket clerk.

"That's him!" He pointed excitedly at Roger. "I knew as soon as he asked for a pencil and started for the john that he was one of those fellows you're looking for!"

The other man, a slight, gray-haired chap with a look of FBI about him, came toward Roger with a knowing smile.

"Have you been, er, decorating the walls, young fellow?" he inquired.

"You've got it all wrong," Roger protested. "I was just—"

"Don't let him go back in and erase them!" the clerk warned.

"The message!" the voice hissed urgently.

"Let's just take a look at your work," the gray-haired man said easily, reaching for the door.

"You don't understand!" Roger backed into the stall. "I was just—"

"Grab him!" The clerk caught his sleeve. The other man caught his other sleeve. As they sought to drag him forth, Roger struggled to free himself from their clutches.

"I'm innocent!" he yelled. "This place was already illustrated when I came in!"

"Yes, of course!" the gray-haired man panted. "Don't get the wrong impression, sir! I'm a curator of the graffiti collection at the Museum of Contemporary Folk Expression. We're looking for creative minds to do a hundred-foot mural for our rotunda!"

With a ripping of cloth, Roger tore free, stumbled back—

"Watch out!" the voice called—too late. Roger saw the shimmering plane flash out on either side, saw it curl in to form a glittering tube about him. For an instant, he teetered there, enclosed in a misty grayness; then, with a sound as of a mighty rushing of waters, he felt himself swirled around and down into depthless emptiness.

CHAPTER TWO

1

He was on a beach. That was the first thought that came into focus as his stunned mind returned to awareness. Brilliant sunshine glared down on yellow sand. He sat up, looked across the shimmer of heat to eroded spires of pink stone looming in the distance. The dance of the air reminded him of something, but thinking made his head hurt. And that in turn reminded him of something else. . . .

Tentatively, Roger Tyson put his hand to his ear, felt the button there.

"Wh-what happened?" he whispered.

There was no answer.

"Voice?" he called. "Agent Q'nell, or whatever your name is?"

Silence.

"Well—at least I'm cured of part of my affliction," Roger told himself. "Now if I can just figure out where I am. . . ." Probably, he considered, he had been on a three-weeks' binge, and was now just coming out of the alcoholic fog.

"Of course, I've never been a drinker," he reminded himself. "But that's probably why it hit me so hard."

He came shakily to his feet, looking around at the vast expanse of sand. It was not a beach, he saw. Merely a boulder-dotted desert, stretching on and endlessly on. "Probably Arizona," he thought. "Maybe the road is just out of sight; but in what direction?"

A massive water-carved rock squatted fifty feet away. Roger went to it, climbed its side. Standing atop it ten feet above the level, he could see for miles across the flat expanse. Far away to the east, a line of pale cliffs edged the world. To the north there was only a vacant horizon. The west was the same. But to the south a ravine cut across the flat ground—and a ravine suggested the action of water.

"A drink," Roger said. "That's what I need." He scrambled down, started across toward the dark line of the cut.

For the first ten minutes he walked steadily forward, skirting the frequent large stones, keeping the sun on his left. Encountering rougher ground, he slowed, picking his route with care.

Mounting a low ridge, he shaded his eyes, scanning the route ahead. The ravine, which should have been very close now, was not to be seen. But . . . Roger closed his eyes, resting them, looked again. What he saw was unmistakable. The boulder that he had climbed, from which he had sighted the ravine, lay a hundred yards ahead, squarely in his path.

2

Four times Roger Tyson had oriented himself with his back to the rock and walked directly away from it—twice to the south, once each to the north and east. Each time, within fifteen minutes, he had returned to the landmark. There had been no careless changes of direction, he was sure of that. Walking east, he had faced directly into the sun's glare—and after a quarter of an hour had again encountered the ubiquitous boulder.

Now he sat in the shade of the massive rock, his eyes closed, feeling the heat that beat down from above, reflected from below, radiated from the stone at his back. Already he felt weak and listless from dehydration. At this rate, he wouldn't last until sundown— the only relief he could hope for. Not that that would change anything. He would still be lost here in this landscape of illusions . . .

That was it! The place didn't really exist; it was nothing but a creation of his fever-racked mind. With this conclusion came a sense that now that he had penetrated the mirage, it should be possible to ignore it. Roger concentrated on the mundane reality of the normal world: singing commercials, tourist attractions, Rotarians, chrome-plated bumpers, artificial eyelashes . . .

He opened his eyes. The lifeless desert still stretched about him. Illusion or otherwise, he was stuck with it.

But damn it, it was impossible! A surge of healthy anger drove him to his feet. There had to be a key to it—some imperfection that could be detected by acute observation. He would pick a starting

point and, step by step, analyze what the situation
was that he faced! This time, sighting on a distant
landmark—a spire of stone at least ten miles away—
Roger walked slowly, pausing frequently to study
the ground around him. He wasn't sure precisely
what he was looking for, but it was clear that the
trap in which he was caught—he thought of it in
those terms now—bore some resemblance to a
goldfish bowl, in which the puzzled fish swam
endlessly, bumping his nose against an invisible
barrier which relentlessly lead him back again to
his starting point. The barrier here was an intangible one, a three-dimensional wall; but like the
glass of the bowl, it should be possible to confront
it directly, rather than sliding along beside it, like
a guppy swimming parallel to the wall of his prison.

Something in the landscape ahead caught Roger's attention, some deviation from the usual aspect of the physical world. It took him minutes of
close observation to pinpoint it: objects in the
distance before him appeared to slide away to left
and right as he advanced. The apparent movement
in itself was a normal perspective effect; it was the
rate of movement that was wrong. The array of
boulders stretching out before him seemed to part
too swiftly—and at the exact center point of his
view, there seemed to be an almost invisible vertical line of turbulence, a line that disappeared as
he halted, resumed again as he went forward,
always at the precise point toward which he moved.
It wasn't a tangible thing, he saw; merely a plane
along which the expansion of the scene took place.
As he watched, a tiny object came into existence
there, grew with each step until the familiar boul-

der lay there in his path, a hundred yards ahead. He looked back. The rock was no longer visible; the distant line of cliffs glowed orange in the late sunlight.

"All right," he said aloud, his voice a lonely sound in the silent immensity around him. "It's some kind of lens effect. A four-dimensional lens, maybe. Putting a name to it doesn't help much, but at least I've pinned down one aspect of it." He scratched a mark on the ground, then walked on to the stone, counting his paces. Three hundred and twenty-one. He returned to the mark, continued along that route until the boulder reappeared ahead; then he went on, counting his steps. Four hundred and four paces in this direction.

"So far, so good," Roger said, walking toward the boulder. "The phenomenon has a fixed center. The fishbowl may be a complete sphere, but it has a definite boundary." He paused as a concept formed in his mind: three-dimensional reality, gathered up at the corners, pulled up to form a closed space, as a washwoman folds up the edges of a sheet to form a bag. . . .

"And all I've got to do," he concluded, "is find the knot!" As this thought completed itself, he noticed a tiny movement ahead. Instantly, he dropped flat behind a convenient rock. Beside the boulder where he had awakened, something glittered in mid-air. Half a dozen metallically jointed members appeared, followed a moment later by a squat, dusky-red body, headless, single-eyed, alien.

"The rutabaga!" Roger choked. "It's still alive—and after me!"

3

Roger lay flat as the monstrous form emerged fully from the empty air, like an actor sliding from behind an invisible flat. It poised for a moment on its clustered supporting members, identical with an upper ring of armlike appendages; then it moved away from the rock, studying the ground ahead.

"It's following my trail!" Roger gulped. "And in five minutes, it will be sneaking up behind me!" He rose to all fours, scuttled forward a few yards, watching the alien creature move rapidly away on flickering tentacles. Darting from cover to cover, he followed it—his only chance, he knew, to stay ahead of it. Approaching the boulder, he saw a tiny glint of light from a vertical line, like a luminous spider's web, extending from the ground upward.

"It's the Aperture!" he gulped in relief. "I hate to reopen the conversation with that art fancier, but it's better than trying to explain to that vegetable how I happened to steal his bike."

Cautiously, Roger edged closer to the luminous filament, saw it widen, close around him as swiftly as a bursting soap bubble, then as swiftly open out again and vanish behind him.

He was standing in darkness, under a sky crisscrossed by glowing arcs, like a Fourth of July display. The air was filled with thunder, punctuated by pops, bangs, and stuttering detonations.

"It's a celebration," Roger guessed, noting that he was standing ankle deep in cold water. "I wonder what the occasion is?" He groped about him, discovered that he was in a muddy, steep-sided ditch higher than his head. A faint glimmer of light reflected from the damp wall of the cut a few feet ahead. He sloshed to it, turned a right-angle corner, and was facing a sand-bagged, timber-braced doorway. Inside, three men sat at a table made of stacked boxes, holding cards. The light came from a candle stuck to a board.

"Hey! You better get inside, buddy!" one of the men called. He was a sallow, thin-faced youth in a mustard-colored jacket, open at the neck. "Big Otto's due to hit any second now!"

"Blimey, mate," a second man, wearing suspenders over wool underwear, said, slapping a card down on the table. "Don't yer know the ruddy schedule?"

The third man, a stout fellow in a gray-green uniform jacket, placed a card on the table and puffed smoke from an enormous pipe.

"Ach, a new *gesicht!*" he exclaimed heartily. *"Bist du vieleicht ein* poker player?"

"Ah—not just now," Roger responded, entering the murky chamber hesitantly. "Say, I wonder if you fellows can tell me where I am? My, uh, car broke down, you see, while I was on my way to apply for a new job. . . ."

Hearty laughter interrupted Roger's explanation.

"New job," the man with the suspenders echoed. "That's a'ot one, chum!"

"Good to meet a guy with a sense o' humor," the man in mustard agreed. "What's your outfit, pal?"

"You are a funny man," the stout player stated solemnly. "You would abbreciate a yoke. *Warum* does *ein Huhn* cross the *strasse?*"

"Outfit?" Roger queried. "I'm afraid I don't have one."

"Wiped out, huh? Too bad. Well, you can doss down here . . ." His voice was drowned by an ear-splitting shriek followed instantly by an explosion that rocked the underground room. The joke-teller reached to flick a smoking fragment of shell casing from the table.

"To come on s' ozzer *seite!*" he said triumphantly. "Also, vun man says to s' ozzer man, 'Who *vass dass* lady I zaw you viss last *nicht?*' "

"What's going on?" Roger blurted, slapping at the mud spattered across his face by the blast.

"The usual Jerry bombardment, o' course, chum. Wot else?"

"Jerry bombardment? You mean—Germans? Good Lord, has a war started?"

"Oh-oh, shell shock," the thin-faced man said. "Too bad. But maybe it's better that way. You get a little variety."

"Where am I?" Roger persisted. "What is this place?"

"You're in good hands, buddy. This is the Saint Mihiel Salient; just take it easy. The shelling will be over in another couple minutes, then we can talk better."

"The Saint Mihiel Salient? B-but that was in World War One!"

"World War what?"

"One. Nineteen eighteen."

"Right, chum. September twelfth. Lousy day, too. I could of picked a better one to be stuck in."

"But—that's impossible! It's nineteen-eighty-seven! You're two wars behind!"

"Crikey—'e's flipped his cap proper," the suspendered man commented.

"Blease! I didn't finish my yoke!" the stout man complained.

"Could it be—is it possible—that the Aperture is some sort of time machine?" Roger gasped.

"Say, buddy, you better get out of the doorway," the thin-faced man suggested. "There's one more big fellow due before it lets up, and—"

"That desert!" Roger blurted. "It wasn't Arizona! It was probably ancient Arabia or something!"

" 'E's raving," The suspender-wearer rose from his seat on an ammunition box. "Watch 'im, mates. 'E might get violent."

"Fantastic!" Roger breathed, looking around the dugout. "Just think, I'm actually back in the past, breathing the air of seventy-odd years ago! Outside, the war is raging, and Wilson's in the White House, and nobody's ever heard of LSD or television or miniskirts or flying saucers—"

"Look, chum, in about ten seconds—"

"You fellows have a lot of excitement to look forward to," Roger said envyingly. "The war will be over in November; try to keep your heads down until then. And afterwards there'll be the League of Nations—that was a failure—and then Prohibition—that didn't work out too well, either— and then the stock market crash in twenth-nine— remember to sell your portfolios early in the year. And then the Great Depression, and then World War Two—"

"Grab him! For 'is own good!"

As the players rose and closed in, Roger backed away. "Now, wait just a minute!" he protested.

"I'm not crazy! It's just that I'm a little confused by what's happened. I have to be going now—"

"You don't hear yet s' punchline!" the stout man protested.

"You'll get y'er bloody 'ead blowed off!"

"Duck, buddy!"

A loud whistle filled the air as Roger broke away and splashed out into the muddy trench. As the sound of the descending shell rose higher and higher he looked both ways for shelter, then dived for the Aperture, saw rainbow light flare about him—

He was sprawled on the grassy bank of a small creek, in full sunlight, looking at a brutal caricature of a man crouched on the opposite side.

4

The man-ape stood all of eight feet tall, in spite of a pronounced stoop; its hands looked as big as catchers' mitts. The shaggy red-brown pelt was matted with dirt, pink scars crossed the wide face, the bronzed, sparsely haired chest. The wide lips drew back on broken, blackened teeth; the small eyes flicked restlessly from Roger to the surrounding woods, back again.

"Oops," Roger murmured. "Wrong era. I'll just nip back through and try that again. . . ."

As he stepped back, the ape-man advanced, splashing down into the stream. Roger forced his way back in among tangled brambles, searching frantically for the glint of light that indicated the exit.

"Maybe it was over more to the left," he suggested, beating his way in that direction. The giant was halfway across the stream now, yelling in indignation at the touch of the water. "Or possibly to the right . . ." Roger clawed at the vines that raked at him like clutching hands. The monster-man emerged from the water, paused to shake first one foot and then the other, then came on, growling ferociously. Roger broke clear of the thicket, skittered away a few feet, and stopped to watch the dull-witted brute entangle itself in the thorny creepers.

"Keep cool, now, Tyson," he counseled. "You can't afford to lose track of the bolthole. Just hover here while that fellow wears himself out, then scoot right in and—"

With a bellow, the ape-man lunged clear of the snarled vines, a move that placed him between Roger and his refuge.

"He—he's probably scared to death," Roger theorized. "All I have to do is act as though I'm not afraid, and he'll turn tail and run." He swallowed hard, adjusted a fierce glint in his eye, and took a hesitant step forward. The result was instantaneous. The creature charged straight at him, seized him with both hands, lifted him clear of the ground. Roger's last impression was of blue sky overhead, seen through a leafy pattern of foliage that whirled around and down and burst into showering lights that faded swiftly into blackness.

CHAPTER THREE

1

He awoke in near-darkness. A pattern of dim light filtered through coarse matting to show him a low ceiling which merged with a wall of water-worn stone. A wizened, bristly-whiskered face appeared, staring down at him. He sat up, winced at the ache in his head; the face retreated hastily. This specimen didn't appear to be vicious—but where was the scar-faced Gargantua?

"Better lie quiet," the old man said in a cracked, whispery voice. "Ye've had a bad bump."

"You speak English!" Roger blurted.

"Reckon I do," the man nodded. "Bimbo had ye, using ye for a play-purty. Ye was lucky he happened to be in a good mood when he found ye. I drug ye in here when he was through with ye."

"Thanks a lot," Roger said. He was discovering new pains with every move. "How did I get this bruise on my side?"

"That was when Bimbo throwed ye down and jumped on ye."

"What happened to my elbow? Both elbows?"

"Must have been when Bimbo was dragging ye around by the heels."

"I guess I lost the hide on my seat at the same time."

"Nope. That was when I hauled ye in here. Too heavy to lift. But don't fret. Tomorrow ain't too far off."

"Glad to see you're a philosopher." Roger's eyes were becoming accustomed to the gloom. The oldster, he saw, was dressed in a dark blue nautical uniform.

"Who are you?" Roger asked. "How did you get here, in the same place with Bimbo?"

"Name's Luke Harwood. Can't rightly say how I got here. Just came ashore to try out my land legs and must of got into some bad rum. Last I remember was heading outside for some fresh air. I woke up here." He sighed. "Guess it's the Lord's punishment for that little business in Macao back in ought nine."

"Would that be . . . nineteen nine?"

"That's it, feller."

"Golly, you don't look that old; but I suppose you were a nipper at the time."

"Well—I sometimes was knowed to take a snort, in good company. But I was never drunk a day in my life. I figger I was hit on the head. Can't rightly say whether I was kilt outright or lingered awhile."

"Where were you when you were, ah, alive?"

"Little place name of Pottsville."

"The same town! But . . . in those days there wasn't any bus station!"

"Don't follow ye there, foller."

"But it was probably the spot where the station was built later! That means the Aperture has been there for years and years! It could be the explanation of some of these mysterious disappearances you hear about, where people step around the corner and are never heard from again."

"I bet they're wondering what become of me," Luke said sadly. "Hardnose Harwood, they used to call me. Set yer watch by me. Never thought I'd end up a ship-jumper."

"Listen, Mr. Harwood, we've got to get out of here."

"Can't do it," Harwood said flatly. "I've tried, lad—many's the time. But there's no way out."

"Certainly there is! The same way you came in! It's down by the river. If you can show me the way to where I met Bimbo . . ."

"You ain't making sense, boy. Once ye're dead and in Purgatory, ye're in for life!"

"I suppose after searching for the exit for sixty years and not finding it, it's hard to believe," Roger conceded, "but—"

"What sixty years?" Harwood frowned.

"The sixty years you've been here, since you arrived as a small boy."

"Ye lost yer rudder, feller? I been here twenty-one days tomorrow!"

"Well—I suppose we can figure that part out later." Roger dismissed the chronology. "But listen—where's Bimbo now?"

"Sleeping off chow in his den down the line, most likely. Bimbo's like the weather: same every day."

"Good; then we'll sneak past him, and—"

"Forget it, feller. Bimbo likes to find things where he left 'em."

"I don't care what he likes! I'm getting out before he kills me. Are you coming, or not?"

"Look here, boy, I taken ye aside to save ye some hard knocks by tipping ye off to the system! If ye know what's good for ye, ye'll—"

"It will be good for me to leave—now," Roger said. "So long, Mr. Harwood. It was nice knowing you."

"Stubborn, ain't ye?" The sailor grunted. "Well, seein's ye're determined, I reckon I'll go along and watch the fun. Now remember—when Bimbo catches ye, don't kick around. That jest riles him."

Stealthily, the two lifted the bamboo mat aside and peered out into the dusty sunshine. The cave, Roger saw, opened onto a rock-strewn ledge above a steep slope shelving down to woodland. It was a long drop; the tops of the great trees barely reached the level of the cave mouth.

Harwood led the way on tiptoe along the ledge. At the entrance to a second, larger cave, he paused, glanced quickly inside.

"Curious," he said. "He ain't here. Wonder where he's at?"

Roger went past him to a sharp angle in the path, edged around it—and was face to face with Bimbo.

"Oh," Harwood said as Roger reappeared around the corner, tucked under the ape-man's shaggy arm. "I see ye found him."

"Don't just stand there!" Roger bleated. "Do something!"

"Thanks for reminding me," Harwood said. He turned and dashed off at top speed. Instantly, Bimbo dropped Roger and lumbered in pursuit. It was a short chase, since the ledge ended after forty feet in a jumble of fallen rock.

"Now, Bimbo"—Harwood scrambled backward, grabbed up a jagged chunk of stone—"ye restrain yerself! Remember last time. That smarted some, didn't it, when I busted ye in the lip?"

Bimbo, unintimidated, closed in, yowled when the thrown missile smacked into his wide face; he grabbed Harwood, and proceded to flail him against the ground. Roger staggered to his feet, caught up a stout length of oak branch, rushed up behind the ape-man, and brought the club down with all his strength on the bullet head. Bimbo ignored the blow, and the three that followed. The fourth seemed to annoy him. He dropped Harwood and whirled. Roger jumped, found a handhold, scrambled up, looked back to see Bimbo's outstretched hand clutch the rock inches from his heels. He kicked at the raking fingers, then scaled another ten feet of rock, pulled himself up onto flat ground. Already Bimbo's rasping breath and scuffling hands were audible just below. Roger looked around hastily for a missile, saw nothing he could use as a weapon. He turned and ran as the furious troll face rose into view.

2

For the first two hundred paces, Roger sprinted at his best speed through open woods directly away from the starting point, careless of noise, acutely aware of Bimbo's crashing progress behind him. In the momentary shelter of a shallow depression, he made a right-angle turn, ran on as silently as possible, emerging after a few hundred feet into open ground with a distant view of mountains. For a moment his heart sank—but in the desert, too, the apparent vista had stretched for miles. He hadn't lost yet. He ran on, conscious of the hopelessness of his exposed position if Bimbo should suspect the change of course too soon.

He was close to exhaustion when he counted off the last few yards of what he hoped would prove to be a closed circle. And there ahead was the hollow where he had changed direction. He dropped flat behind a bush to catch his breath, listening to the sounds of breaking brush and the hoarse bellows of the frustrated Bimbo threshing about in the underbrush well off to the right. His wind recovered, Roger retraced his steps to the bluff above the cave. Below, a dozen heavy, shaggy half-men had emerged from concealment. They stood in a ragged circle around Luke Harwood, who was sitting up, holding his side.

Roger swung over the edge, scrambled quickly down to the ledge. At sight of him, the brute-men scattered, disappearing into the innumerable hollows in the rock. With the exception of Bimbo, it appeared, the brutal appearance of the creatures concealed timorous natures. Hardwood tottered to his feet, dusty and disheveled, dabbing ineffectually at a bloody nose.

"Ye shouldn't have done it, lad! He hates to have anybody interfere with him when he's having fun!"

"I missed a swell chance to finish him," Roger said between gasps of breath. "I should have climbed up and rolled a rock down on him."

"Ahhh," Harwood demurred. "Killing him *really* gets his dander up. I killed him three times before I gave it up. If ye'd squashed him I dread to think o' the consequences. Now, give yerself up, man! Wait here and take what comes like a man! It can't last forever—though he's learned to be sly about it, to stretch it out till sundown. But tomorrow will come at last, and unless ye've angered him beyond measure, he'll have forgot by then!"

"Never mind tomorrow. Come on; I've thrown him off the scent for the moment."

A hoarse bellow sounded from the clifftop above.

"He's found yer trail," Harwood hissed. "Ye're in for it—unless . . ." There was speculation in his eyes. "Down by the creek, ye say?"

"Which way down?" Roger snapped.

"Come along," Harwood said. "I guess I owe ye that much."

3

Five minutes later Roger and Harwood stood beside the small stream which flowed through the wooded ground below the cliff, all that remained of the mighty flow which, ages ago, had carved the gorge.

"There was a nice stand of timber at the spot I'm looking for," Roger said. "A big elm, a yard in diameter, about ten feet from the bank—"

"White pebbles in the bottom?" Harwood cut in.

"I think so . . . yes."

"This way."

The sound of Bimbo's crashing approach came clearly to their ears as they hurried along the bank. It was no more than a minute before Roger halted, looking around.

"This is the place," he said. "I was right at the water's edge, with a big pine at my back." He stepped to the tree, pulled aside the low-growing boughs, squinting into deep shade.

"I don't see nothing," Harwood muttered. "Looky, if we go back now and give ourselves up, maybe it'll take the edge off his temper."

"It's here," Roger said. "It's got to be here!"

"I don't know about that," Harwood said. "But Bimbo's here!"

"Keep him occupied!" Roger urged as the giant burst into view, puffing like a switch engine.

"Sure." Harwood's tone was not without an edge of sarcasm. "I'll trick him into pulling my legs off one at a time; that'll hold his attention fer a minute or two."

Suddenly there was a crackling of twigs and a swishing of leaves to Roger's left. A pair of segmented metallic tubes were groping about as though testing the air. A bulge of dusty red swelled into view, followed by the remainder of the headless body of the monster Roger had last seen in the desert.

"Cornered!" Roger gasped. "And I was so close . . ."

The alien being swiveled its lone eye about, failed to notice Roger lurking in the shadowy greenery. It pushed forward, emerged onto the riverbank a few feet behind Luke Harwood, who was making pushing motions toward the advancing Bimbo. The latter paused, his tiny red eyes flicking from the men to the monster, which stood jouncing on its spidery legs, waving its upper members uncertainly. The motion appeared to annoy Bimbo; he bellowed and charged straight past the astonished Harwood and on into the foliage as the alien bounded aside.

"Luke! This way!" Roger yelled as he lunged for the Aperture. Harwood, imagining the ape-man to be on his heels, sprang for the cover offered. Roger caught his arm, dragged him with him toward the line of light, which widened, flashed around the pair, and vanished as darkness closed in.

4

"Land sakes!" Luke muttered. "Where in tarnation are we?"

"I don't know—but at least there's no shellfire," Roger said. He felt around him, sniffled, shuffled his feet. He was standing on a hard-surfaced road, under a starry night sky. Wind moved softly in treetops; a cricket shrilled. Far away a train hooted sorrowfully.

"Hey—a light!" Luke pointed.

"Maybe it's a house," Roger said. "Maybe . . . maybe we're Outside!"

"Yippee," Luke caroled. "Just wait'll the boys back on the poop deck hear about this! Ye reckon they'll believe me?"

"You'd better prepare for a shock," Roger said. "Frankly, there've been a few changes . . ."

"Trouble is, I got no proof," Luke said. "In the last three weeks I had two broken arms, a busted leg, six split lips, goshamighty knows how many busted ribs and bruises, lost six teeth, and been beat to death four times—and not even a blood blister to prove it!"

"You'll have to curb your tendency to exaggerate," Roger said. "We might be able to sell our story to the newspapers for a tidy sum, but not if you carry on like that."

"Funny thing is," Luke said, "there ain't nothing much to it—getting kilt, I mean. Just blap! And then you're waking up and starting all over."

"I suppose Bimbo is enough to unhinge anybody," Roger muttered sympathetically. "But let's not think about that part now, Mr. Harwood. Let's go find a telephone and start shopping around for a publisher."

Five minutes' walk brought them to the source of the gleam. It was a lighted window in a converted farmhouse, standing high and white above a slope of black lawn. The two men followed the flower-bordered drive—two strips of concrete, somewhat cracked but still serviceable—to a set of brick steps leading up onto the wide porch. Roger knocked. There was no response. He knocked again, louder. This time he thought he heard uncertain footsteps.

"Who . . . who's there?" a frightened female voice came from inside.

"My name is Tyson, ma'am," Roger called to the closed door. "I wonder if I might use your phone?"

A bolt clicked; the door opened half an inch. A

woman's face appeared—at least one large, dark eye and the tip of her nose. For a moment she stared at him; then the door swung back. The woman—slim, middle-aged, still pretty—swayed as if she were about to fall. Roger stepped quickly forward, caught her elbow.

"Are you all right?"

"Yes—I—I—I—it's just . . . I thought . . . I was the only one left in the world!" She collapsed into his arms, weeping hysterically.

5

Half an hour later, their hostess restored to calm, they were seated at a table in the kitchen, sipping hot coffee and exchanging reports.

"So—I just settled down and made the best of it," Mrs. Withers said. "I guess it's been the most restful three months of my life."

"How have you managed?" Roger asked. "I mean for food."

Mrs. Withers went to the brown wooden icebox, opened it.

"Every morning it's full again," she said. "The same things: the three slices of ham, the half-dozen eggs, the bottle of milk, some lettuce, leftovers. And there are the canned goods. I've eaten the same can of creamed corn forty times." A smile twitched at her face. "Luckily, I like creamed corn."

"And the ice?" Roger pointed at the half-melted block in the bottom compartment.

"It melts every day and every morning it's whole again. And the flowers: I cut them every day and bring them in and the next morning they're back outside, growing on the same stems. And once I cut myself on a can. It was a deep cut, but in the morning it was gone, not even a scar. At first, I tore a page off the calendar every day, but it came back. It never changes, you see. Nothing changes. The sky is the same, the same weather, even the same clouds. It's always the same day: August seventeenth, nineteen thirty-one."

"Actually . . ." Roger began.

"Skip it, son," Luke whispered behind his hand. "If she gets any comfort out of thinking it's twenty-two years in the future, let her."

"What would you say if I told you it was nineteen eighty-seven?"

"I'd say your mainstay's parted, son."

"I'd argue with you," Roger said. "Except that I wouldn't want my suspicions along those lines confirmed."

"What's happened, Mr. Tyson? What does it mean?" Mrs. Withers asked.

"We've fallen into a trap of some sort," Roger said. "It may be a natural phenomenon or an artificial one, but it has rules and limitations. We already know a few of them."

"Yes," Mrs. Withers nodded. "You *did* come here—from somewhere. Can we go back?"

"You wouldn't like it there," Roger said. "But I don't think we'll land in the same place. I haven't so far. There seems to be a series of these cages, all joined at one point—a sort of fourth-dimensional manifold. When we leave here, we'll probably step into another cell. But I'm hoping we'll eventually find ourselves outside."

"Mr. Tyson—may . . . may I go with you?"

"You can come along if you like," Roger agreed.

"I want to," Mrs. Withers said. "But you *will* wait until morning?"

"I'll be glad of a night's sleep," Roger sighed. "I can't remember the last one I had."

Lying in a clean bed in a cozy room half an hour later, Roger looked at his watch. 12:20. There was no reason, of course, to expect that an arbitrarily designated midnight should have any special significance in terms of the physical laws now governing things, but nonetheless . . .

Time blinked.

There had been no physical shock, no sound, no change in the light. But *something* had happened. At 12:21 precisely, Roger noted the time. He looked around the room, in the almost total darkness saw nothing out of the ordinary. He went to the bed where Luke Harwood lay, bent to look at the man's face.

The scratches were gone. Roger touched his own bruised side, winced.

"It's a closed cycle, in time as well as space," he murmured. "Everything reverts to the state it was in twenty-four hours earlier—all but me. I'm different; my bruises collect. That being the case, let's hope tomorrow is an easier day than this one."

CHAPTER FOUR

1

Bright and early the following morning, the trio left the house carrying a small paper bag of food and a twenty-two-caliber rifle Mrs. Withers had produced along with three cartridges. Roger located the Aperture after a short search.

"We'd better stay close together," he said. "I suggest we hold hands, just to be sure we don't get separated and wind up in different localities."

Mrs. Withers offered a hand to each of her two escorts. Roger in the lead, they stepped forward—

—and emerged in deep twilight which gleamed on giant conifers spreading ice-crusted boughs in the stillness. Roger sank calf deep in the soft snow. The air was bitterly cold.

"That was a short day," Luke grunted. "Let's go back and try again."

"I should have thought of this," Roger said. "It must be below zero."

"I'll just run back and get coats," Mrs. Withers suggested.

"It doesn't work that way," Roger said. "We may wind up in a worse place than this. And while we're here, we may as well look around. For all we know, we're clear. There may be a road within fifty feet of us, a house just over the rise! We can't run away without even looking. Luke, you go that way"—he pointed up-slope—"and I'll check below. Mrs. Withers, you wait here. We'll be right back."

Luke nodded, looking unhappy, started off in the direction indicated. Roger patted the woman's arm and set off among the trees. Already, his hands and toes and ears ached as if pliers were clamped on them. His breath formed instantly into fog before his face. He had gone no more than a hundred feet when he saw the felled tree.

It was a small pine, a foot in diameter at the base, only lightly powdered with snow. Most of the branches had been trimmed off and were neatly stacked nearby. The stump was cleanly cut, as if by a sharp axe. Roger studied the ground for tracks, in a moment found them, partially filled by blown snow.

"Only a few hours old," he muttered half aloud. The tracks led directly up-slope. He started off, following them, not an easy task in the failing light. He had almost reached the ridge when the deep *boom!* of a gun shattered the arctic stillness.

For a moment Roger stood rigid, listening as the echoes of the single shot rang in the air. It had come from the right, the direction Luke Harwood had taken. He started off at a run. The drifted snow caught at his legs, dragging at him; the icy air burned in his throat. He fell back to a walk, scanning the shadowy forest all around for signs of life, detoured around a giant fallen tree, encountered deeper snow. He heard faint sounds of movement ahead, as of someone hurrying away through the snow.

"Wait!" Roger called, but his voice was only a weak croak. For an instant, panic gripped him, but he forced it down.

"Got to get out," he whispered. "Colder than I thought. Freezing. Find Luke, get back to Mrs. Withers . . ."

He stumbled on, his hands and feet numb now, forced his way through a tangle of dry, ice-coated brush, and saw a crumpled figure lying in the snow. It was Luke Harwood, lying on his back, a bullet hole in his chest, his sightless eyes already rimmed with frost.

2

There was nothing he could do for Luke, Roger saw. He turned and set off at a stumbling run for the spot where he had left Mrs. Withers. Ten minutes later he realized he was lost. He stood in the gathering dusk, staring about at ranks of identical trees. He shouted, but there was no answer.

"Poor Mrs. Withers," he thought, his teeth chattering. "I hope she goes back through before she freezes to death." He stumbled on a little farther. Then without remembering falling, he was lying softly cradled in the snow. The warm, cozy snow. All he had to do was curl up here and snooze a

while, and later . . . when he was rested . . .
try . . . again.

3

He awoke lying in a bed beside a hide-covered
window aglow with watery daylight. A tall, gaunt,
bearded man was standing over him, chewing his
lower lip.

"Well, you're awake," Job Arkwright said. "Where
was you headed anyways, stranger?"

"I . . . I . . . I . . ." Roger said. His hands and
feet and nose hurt, but otherwise he seemed sound
of mind and limb. "What happened? Who are
you? How did I get here?" A sudden thought
struck him. "Where is Mrs. Withers?"

"Your missus is all right. She's asleep." The
gaunt man nodded toward a bunk above the one in
which Roger lay.

"Say!" Roger sat bolt upright. "Are you the one
that shot Luke?"

"Reckon so. Sorry about that. Friend o' yours, I
s'pose. I took him for somebody else."

"Why?" Roger blurted.

"Reckon it was the bad light."

"I mean—why were you going to shoot somebody else?"

"Why, heck, I never even met your friend to
talk to, much less shoot, leastwise on purpose."

"I mean—oh, never mind. Poor Luke. I wonder
what his last thoughts were, all alone out in the
snow."

"Dunno. Why don't you ast him?" The stranger

stepped back and Luke Harwood stood there, grinning down at Roger.

"B-but you're dead!" Roger yelped. "I saw you myself! There was a hole in you as big as your thumb!"

"Old Betsy's bite's as mean as her bark," Arkwright said proudly. "You should of seed Fly Beebody, time I picked him out of a pine at a hundred yards. One of my finest shots. He'll be along any minute now; get him to tell you about it."

"I told ye getting killed don't mean shucks," Luke said. "Job here done a clean job, never smarted a bit."

Roger flopped back with a groan. "I guess that means we're still stuck in the trap."

"Yes. But it could of been worse. At least Job here drug us inside out of the weather. I figger in your case, that saved yer skin."

There was a thumping at the door. A slim woman Roger hadn't noticed before opened it to admit a plump young fellow with a bundlesome overcoat and a resentful expression.

"The least thee could do, Brother Arkwright, would be to lay me out in Christian style after thee shoots me," he said as the woman took his coat and shook the snow from it.

"Don't like to see the remains cluttering up the place," Job said carelessly. "You ought to be thankful I let you in next morning."

"You mean—you actually shot that man?" Roger whispered hoarsely. "Intentionally?"

"Dern right. Caught him making up to Charity," he added in a lower tone. "That's my woman.

Good cook, but flighty. And Fly's got a eye for tho skinny ones. He goes along for a few days holding hisself under control, and then one day he busts loose and starts praising her corn meal mush, and I know it's time to teach him another lesson."

"How long has this been going on?"

"All winter. And it's been a blamed long winter, I'll tell you, stranger."

"Poor fellow! It must be ghastly for him!"

"Oh, I dunno. Sometimes he puts one over on me and gets me first. But he's a mighty poor shot. Plugged Charity once, by mistake, jist like I plugged your sidekick."

"Bloodcurdling!"

"Oh, Charity gets in her licks, too. She nailed the both of us once. Didn't care for it, though, she said afterward. Too lonesome. Now she alternates."

"You mean—she's likely to shoot you without notice—just like that?"

"Yep. But I calculate a man's got to put up with a few little quirks in a female."

"Good Lord!"

"Course, I don't much cotton to the idea of what goes on over my dead body—but I guess, long as she's a widder, it don't rightly count."

Charity Arkwright approached with a steaming bowl on a tray.

"Job, you go see to the kindling whilst I feed this nice young man some gruel," she said, giving Roger a bright smile.

"Thanks, anyway," Roger said quickly, recoiling. "I'm allergic to all forms of gruel."

"Look here, stranger," Job growled. "Charity's a good cook. You ought to try a little."

"I'm sure she's wonderful," Roger gulped. "I just don't want any."

"That sounds mighty like a slur to me, stranger!"

"No slur intended! It's just that I had a bad experience with my oatmeal as a child, and ever since I've been afraid to try again!"

"I bet I could help you with your problem," Charity offered, looking concerned. "The way I do it, it just melts in your mouth."

"Tell you what, Miz Charity," Luke Harwood put in. "I'll take a double helping—just to show ye ye're appreciated."

"Don't rush me, mister!" Charity said severely. "I'll get around to you when it's your turn!"

"Hey, stranger," Job said. "Your missus is awake; reckon she'd like some?"

"No! She hates the stuff!" Roger said, scrambling out of bed to find himself clad only in ill-fitting long johns. "Give me my clothes! Luke, Mrs. Withers, let's get out of here!"

"Now, hold on, partner! You're the first variety we've had around this place in shucks knows how long! Don't go getting huffy jist over a little breakfast food!"

"It's not the food—it's the prospect of getting to know Betsy better. Besides which, we started out to find a way out of this maze, not just to settle down being snowbound!"

"I swan," Charity said. "And me the finest gruelmaker west of the Missouri! Never thought I'd see the day when I couldn't give it away!"

"Mister, I reckon you got a few things to learn about frontier hospitality," Job said grimly, lifting a wide-mouth muzzle-loader down from above the door and aiming it at Roger's chin. "I don't reckon nobody ain't leaving here until they've at least tried it."

"I'm convinced," Luke said.

"How do you like it?" Charity inquired. "Plain, or with sugar and cream?"

"Goodness, what's all this talk about gruel?" Mrs. Withers inquired from her bunk, sitting up. "I've got a good mind to show you my crêpes suzettes."

"I never went in for none of them French specialties," Job said doubtfully. "But I could learn."

"Well, I like that!" Charity snapped. "I guess plain old country style's not good enough any more!"

"Well," Mrs. Withers said. "If it's all you can get . . ."

"Why, you scrawny little city sparrer!" Charity screeched, and leaped for the rival female. Roger yelled and lunged to intercept her. Job Arkwright's gun boomed like a cannon; the slug caught Charity under the ribs and hurled her across the room.

"Hey! I never meant—" That was as far as Arkwright got. The boom of a two-barreled derringer in the hands of Fly Beebody roared out. The blast knocked the bearded man backward against the door, which flew open under the impact, allowing him to pitch backward into the snow. As Roger staggered to his feet, a baroque shape loomed in the opening. Metallic tentacles rippled, bearing a rufous tuber shape, one-eyed, many-armed, into the cabin.

"Help!" Roger shouted.

"Saints preserve us!" Luke yelled.

"Beelzebub!" squealed Fly Beebody, and fired

his second round into the alien body at point-
blank range. The bullet struck with a fruity *smack!*,
spattering carroty material; but the creature turned,
apparently unaffected, fixed his immense ocular
on the parson. It rippled toward him, grasping
members outstretched.

Roger grabbed a massive hand-hewn chair, swung
it up, and brought it down with tremendous force
atop the blunt upper end of the monstrosity. It
toppled under the blow, rolled in a short arc like
an overturned milk bottle, threshed its tentacles
briefly, and was still.

"Now will you leave?" Roger inquired in the
silence.

"I'll go with thee!" Beebody yelped. "Satan has
taken over this house in spite of my prayers!"

"We can't leave this thing here," Roger said.
"We'll have to take it along; otherwise it will be
the first thing to greet them in the morning!" He
took a blanket from the bed and rolled the creature
in it.

"Best ye stay here, girl," Luke said to Mrs.
Withers. "Lord knows what we'll run into next."

"Stay here—with *them?*"

"They'll be themselves again tomorrow."

"That's what I'm afraid of!"

"Well, then; ye better don Charity's cloak."

"We'll leave the coats at the Aperture," Roger
said. "In the morning, they'll be back here."

"I'll leave the can of soup," Mrs. Withers said as
they prepared to step out into the sub-zero night.
"I think Mr. Arkwright was getting a little tired of
the same old gruel."

Outside, the wind struck at Roger's frost-nipped

face like a spiked board. He pulled his borrowed muffler up around his ears, hefted his end of the shrouded alien, led the way up into the dark forest, following tracks made earlier that morning by Luke.

It was a fifteen-minute hike through blowing snow to the spot among the trees where they had arrived. All of them except Beebody stripped off their heavy outer garments; Roger took the blanket-sack over his shoulder, held Mrs. Withers' hand, while Luke and Beebody joined to form a shivering line, like children playing a macabre game.

"Too bad we couldn't even leave them a note," Roger said. He approached the faint-glowing line, which widened, closed in about him, and opened out into brilliant sunlight on a beach of red sand.

CHAPTER FIVE

1

Fly Beebody hunkered on his knees, his fingers interlaced, babbling prayers in a high, shrill voice. Luke stood staring around curiously. Mrs. Withers stood near him, still shivering, hugging herself. Roger dumped his burden at his feet, savoring the grateful heat. The sun, halfway to zenith, glared blindingly on choppy blue water, sand, and rock.

"No signs of life," Luke said. "Where would ye say we are, Roger?"

"That's hard to say. In the tropics, apparently. But what part of the tropics is as barren as this?"

He knelt, studied the sandy ground. "No weeds, no insects." He walked down across the loose sand to the water's edge, bent, and scooped up water in his hand and tasted it. It was curiously flat and insipid. No fish swam in the shallows, no moss grew on the rocks, no seaweed drifted on the tide.

"No seashells," he called. "Just a little green scum on the water." As he turned to start back, he became suddenly aware of the sunlight beating down at him, the drag of gravity. He sucked air into his lungs, fighting a sense of suffocation that swept over him. Ahead, Fly Beebody's chanting had broken off; he half rose, bundlesome in the blanket coat, his mouth opening and closing like a fish's. Luke was struggling to support the widow, who sagged against him. Roger broke into a stumbling run.

"Back!" he called. "Get back through! Bad air!" He reached the group, caught the woman's limp hand.

"Grab Beebody's hand!" he gasped to Harwood. He caught up the bundle. As his vision began to fade into a whirling fog of flickering lights, he groped forward, found the Aperture, half-fell through it.

2

He lay in warm, foul-smelling water, his arms buried to the elbows in soft muck, breathing in great lungfuls of humid, steaming air. A dragonfly with gauzy, foot-long wings hovered a yard away among the finger-thick stems of giant cattails, buzzing like an electric fan. As he sat up, it darted away, eerie, pre-storm sunlight glinting on its polished green body. Beside him, Luke struggled to his feet, black with reeking mud, dragged Mrs. Withers upright. Beebody floundered, spitting sulphurous water.

Standing among reeds higher than his head, Roger could see nothing but more of the same, stretching away endlessly in all directions.

"This must be an era between periods of mountain building," he said. "There was very little dry land on the planet then. I suppose we're lucky we didn't end up treading deep water."

There was a sudden splash near at hand, a sound of violent threshing in the water. The source was invisible through the screen of reeds, but spray flew up from a point twenty feet away and ripples moved toward the sodden travelers. A deep hoot sounded, like a breathy foghorn. The sounds of struggle grew louder, closer. As Roger floundered toward the portal, a finned snake as big around as his thigh burst into view, wrapped around and around a short-snouted crocodile whose jaws were clamped hard in the sinuous body. The struggling pair threshed through the reeds in a churn of crimsoned water. Roger jumped for the ribbon of light, pulling Mrs. Withers after him. There was the flash of prismatic color—

—then a cold rain was driving at him, swirled into his face by a gusty wind. Through the whirling sheets of water, a cluster of sagging, irregularly shaped tents was visible, their sodden leather coverings, marked with crude symbols, whipping in the wind.

"This doesn't look promising," Luke shouted above the sounds of the storm. "I say let's move on without waiting to get acquainted."

"Why be hasty?" Roger countered. "For all we know, we're outside—" He broke off as a bearded, dark-faced man thrust his head from the nearest tent flap. For a moment their eyes met; then the man plunged, grabbing for a short, curved sword slung at his side, and advanced, yelling.

By common assent, the party joined hands and plunged back through the shimmering barrier.

3

They were on a great veldt, where endless herds of game grazed and vultures circled overhead. Luke and Mrs. Withers stood by the Aperture to mark it while Roger and Beebody, the latter still bundled, sweating in his coat, walked away through the sea of chest-high grass.

Fifteen minutes later, they approached the same spot from behind.

"Still trapped," Roger said. "Let's go on."

They passed . . . through—

—and were . . . on a mountainside above a wide valley with a lake far below. They went on, found themselves on a wide tundra, where far away a pair of huge, shaggy animals lumbered, head-down, into the biting wind. Next, they splashed knee-deep in cold water, near a guano-whitened headland where seabirds circled, crying. After that, there was a dry, brush-choked gorge that led back onto itself when Roger explored its twisting length. Then a bamboo thicket beside a wide, muddy river, under a gray, humid sky.

"It's a marvel how much dreary landscape the world has to offer," Luke panted after a quarter of an hour of splashing through the shallows had led them back to their starting point.

"We'll have to try again," Roger said. "We can't stay here." He swatted one of the huge, inquisitive mosquitoes that swarmed about their heads. They stepped once more through the Aperture—

—and were . . . in a wide field of flowers, under a balmy sky. All around, wooded hills rose to an encircling ring of snow-capped peaks. A small falls tumbled down over a rocky outcropping nearby, feeding a clear river that wound off across the plain.

"How beautiful!" Mrs. Withers exclaimed. "Roger — Luke—can't we stay here awhile?"

"I'm wearied with this scrambling from one climate to the next," Luke agreed. "And we're no closer to escape than ever."

"It suits me," Roger said. "And I'm hungry. Let's get a fire going and rustle a meal."

After they ate, Mrs. Withers wandered off, picking the crimson poppies and yellow buttercups that abounded there, accompanied, grumbling, by Luke. Roger stretched out on the grass by the Aperture, Beebody squatting uncomfortably beside him.

"Master Roger," the parson said awkwardly after the others had passed out of earshot. "I . . . I propose that we come to terms, thee and me."

"About what?"

Beebody hunkered closer. "As thee see, thy strength avails naught against mine. Try as thee will to draw my soul into Hell, still I resist, sustained by prayer and righteousness."

"Try to get this, Beebody," Roger said. "As far as I'm concerned, you can keep your soul. All I want is a way out of here."

"Aye—a path back into the Pit thee came from!"

Beebody hissed. "Think thee not I can smell the
brimstone on thee—and on the imp who takes the
form of Luke? Did I not mark how thee two stood
against thy fellow demon, sent no doubt by thee to
slay Job Arkwright and his mistress." His eyes
went to the bundle. "And think thee not I understand why thee was so set on bearing the foul
remains of thy ally with us?"

"Go to sleep, Fly," Roger said. "You'll need all
the rest you can get."

"I have prayed and meditated, even as by the
strength of my virtue I kept thee from the path
thee seek; and it comes to me now that, to preserve
my earthly husk to continue the struggle against sin,
it would be meet to come to agreement with thee.
Otherwise will we both exhaust ourselves."

"Come to the point," Roger said roughly. "What
do you want?"

"Take the woman," Beebody whispered. "Spare
me! Return me to the true world, and I'll omit
thee in my curses!"

"You're an amazing man, Fly," Roger said, studying the cherubic face, the worried eyes. "Suppose
I take you, and free Odelia instead?"

"Nay, demon, my works are needed in the sin-
ful world of fallen man! I cannot allow such a
victory to the Dark One!"

"Your concern for the populace is touching,"
Roger said, "but—" He broke off as Fly Beebody's
eyes went past him, widening. The fat man rose to
his feet, pointing. Roger turned to look. A shaggy
brown bear had appeared at the edge of the forest,
a hundred feet distant. It moved forward confi-
dently, directly toward the two men.

"I yield!" Beebody babbled. "Send not this new devil to me! I consent to join with thee, to aid thee in thy fell designs! Take the woman! I'll help thee now! I'll fight thee no longer!"

"Shut up, you jackass!" Roger snapped. "Luke!" he called. "Get Mrs. Withers through the Aperture!"

Luke and Mrs. Withers started back at a run. The bear, interested in the activity, broke into a heavy gallop. "Beebody!" Roger shouted. "Help me distract him until they're clear!" From the corner of his eye, he saw the parson move—in the opposite direction. He turned in time to see him lift the bagged alien, swing the bulky bundle toward the Aperture.

"Fly! Don't! You might be dumping that monster in among defenseless people!" Roger grabbed for the blanket, but Beebody resisted with surprising strength. For a moment they struggled back and forth, Beebody red of face and rattling off appeals to a Higher Power, Roger casting looks over his shoulder at the rapidly approaching animal, and at Luke and Odelia Withers, coming up fast from the right.

Suddenly his foot slipped. He felt himself whirled about, off balance. He tottered back, saw the glint of the Aperture expanding around him, saw Beebody's flushed face, Luke and the woman behind him, and beyond, the open jaws of the bear.

The daylight winked out—

—to be replaced by an all-enclosing gray. For an instant, Roger teetered on one toe, struggling for balance. Then a giant hand closed on his body, yanked him up, around, and out into the brilliant light of a vast, white-floored room.

4

He stood half-dazed, staring around at looming banks of gleaming apparatus under a glowing ceiling that arched overhead like an opaque sky, hearing the soft hum and whine of machinery that filled the air. Nearby stood half a dozen sharp-eyed men with excellent physiques shown off by form-fitting outfits in various tasteful colors.

One of the men stepped forward, emitted a sharp, burping sound, looking at Roger warningly.

"I hear the Asiatics do that after dinner," Roger said in a tone close to hysteria. "But I never heard of using it as a greeting."

"Hmmm. Pattern noted: Subject either fails to understand, or pretends to fail to understand Speedspeak. I will therefore employ Old Traditional." He eyed Roger sternly. "I was just advising you that disorganizer beams are focused on you. Make no attempt to employ high-order mental powers, or we will be forced to stimulate your pain centers to level nine or above."

"B-b-b-b," Roger said.

"Your behavior has puzzled us," the man went on in a cool, mellow voice. "We have followed your path through the Museum. It appears aimless. Since this is incompatible with your identity, it follows that your motives are of an order of complexity not susceptible to cybernetic analysis. It therefore becomes necessary to question you. It is for this reason that we have taken the risk of grappling you from the Channel."

"My m-motives?" Roger gulped. "Look here, you fellows have got the wrong idea."

"You continue to broadcast meaningless images of flight and primitive fear," his inquisitor stated. "These delaying tactics will not be tolerated." A swift flash of pain tingled along Roger's bones.

"What was the principle underlying your choice of route?" the questioner demanded.

"There wasn't any!" Roger yelped as the pain nipped him again.

"Hmmm. His movements *do* fit in with a random factor of the twelfth order," a second man spoke up. "It appears the situation is more complex than we imagined."

"His appearance here at this particular juncture is a most provocative datum," another pointed out. "It suggests a surveillance aspect we've failed heretofore to include in our computations."

"He's obviously an incredibly tough individual, capable of enduring any mere psychophysical stimulus without breaking," a man in powder blue contributed. "Otherwise he would never have been dispatched on his errand—whatever that might be."

"In that case, we may as well proceed at once to mechanical mind-stripping techniques," a lemon-yellow Adonis proposed. There was a soft *click!* and a large, white-enameled, blunt-snouted machine like a gigantic dentist's drill swung into position directly over Roger.

"Wait a minute!" he protested, and attempted to back away, only to discover that he was paralyzed—rooted to the spot. "What's the big idea?" he blurted. "Let me out of here! For all you know, I had important business pending back where I came from! I might have been on my way to land a high-pay, low-work job! I could have been rushing to marry the richest and most beautiful woman in the Middle West! I might even have been on my way to Washington to deliver information vital to the national security!"

"What a mind-shield!" a man in raspberry pink said admiringly, studying his dials. "If I didn't know better, I'd swear he was only a high-grade moron with an IQ scarcely above one hundred forty."

"That's it!" Roger agreed. "Now we're getting somewhere! I don't know who you gentlemen think I am, but I'm not! I'm Roger Tyson, gentleman adventurer—"

"Come now," the man in blue said kindly. "Do you expect us to believe that your appearance in the Museum today—if you'll pardon the expression-just as we are about to launch our long-awaited probe mission down the null-temporal Axis is sheer coincidence?"

"Absolutely," Roger said fervently. "As a matter of fact, I haven't the faintest idea where I am now. Or"—a look of dawning wonder appeared on his face—"*when* I am!"

"Our era is the twenty-third decade after the Forcible Unification. About twenty-two forty-nine, Old Calendar—as if you didn't know."

"Three hundred years in the future?" Roger's voice failed. He swallowed a golf ball that had lodged in his throat. "I guess it figures. I should have known—"

"We wander afield, S'lunt," a man in deep purple interrupted. "Jump-off hour approaches. Now, quickly, fellow! What was your mission?"

There was a small stir at the edge of the circle of men, but Roger scarcely noticed, due to a sensation like an aching tooth centered in the small of his back.

"Explain the nature of the binding forces subsumed in the Rho complex!"

A heavy boot trod on the tip of a long tail Roger had never suspected he possessed.

"Define the nature and alignment matrices of the pulse guides!"

A blunt saw amputated Roger's antlers. The horns, he saw, squinting upward through a haze of pain, were imaginary, but the attendant sensations were vividly real.

"Enumerate the coordinate systems postulated in the syllogistical manipulations, and specify the axial rotations employed!"

A wrecker's ball swung from somewhere and flattened him to a thin paste.

"Hmmm. I have a feeling this entire procedure is illegal, under the provisions of Spool Nine Eighty-Seven of the Social Motivation Code!" someone whispered in Roger's ear.

"I demand a lawyer!" Roger squalled.

"Eh?" the man in blue inquired. He turned to his chartreuse-clad associate. "R'heet, run a quick semantic analysis of that utterance, in the fourth and twelfth modes, with special attention to connotational resonances of the second category."

"This whole thing is illegal!" Roger yelled. "Under Spool, uh, Nine Eighty-Seven of the Social, uh, Motivation Code!"

"How's that?" The man called S'lunt eyed Roger sharply. "How do you know of the Code?"

"*What difference does that make?*" the voice hissed. "*Illegal is illegal!*"

"What does that matter?" Roger echoed. "Illegal is illegal!"

"Why, er, as to that . . ."

"*Just because we're faced with an emergency, there's no reason to stoop to totalitarian techniques!*"

"That's right," Roger nodded vigorously. "Just because there's an emergency, is no reason to act like Hitler!"

"I don't know, S'lunt," the pink-garbed dial watcher said. "These readings are persistently in the retarded sector. I have a sneaking suspicion we may have made a mistake."

"You mean—he's *not* an agent of the Entity?"

"Of course not!" Roger shouted. "I'm just a poor wayfaring stranger named Roger Tyson!"

"In that case, why did he register so strongly on our gamitron detectors?"

"*Maybe the varpilators need adjusting.*"

"Better check your varpilators," Roger said quickly.

"Say—that's a thought—but—"

"*And while you're at it, you might just realign the transfrication rods.*"

"And take a look at the transfrication rods!"

"See here, you seem to know a great deal about Culture One technical installations," S'lunt said accusingly.

"*Maybe you're from our future, and have an interest in history.*"

"That's right, how do you know I'm not from the future, hah?"

"Say—in that case, he could tell us what's going to happen next back home!"

"Gad! What an exciting prospect!" S'lunt said eagerly. "Tell me, sir, how did General Minerals do on the big board in fifty?"

"Did that intelligent slime-mould on Venus turn out to be alive?"

"Did they ever get the LBJ Memorial Asteroid towed out of the Mars-Terra space lane?"

"It's kind of hard for me to remember while I'm paralyzed with my neck at this angle," Roger pointed out.

"Dear me, forgive me, sir!" S'lunt flicked a switch and Roger felt himself unfreeze.

"R'heet, get our guest a chair. How about a little draught of medicinal alcohol, sir?"

"Thanks; don't mind if I do." Roger accepted the libation, sank into the seat, which squirmed sensually, adapting itself to his contours.

"Now, you were saying about the election of flfty-two . . .?"

"The, ah, dark horse won," Roger improvised. "By the way, how about letting me out of this place now?"

"Did the Immortality Bill pass?"

"By a landslide. If you don't mind I'd like to just be dropped at the edge of town—any town."

"By george, what did Alpha Expedition Three report?"

"Dense fog," Roger replied tersely. "And if it's all the same to you, I'd like to get going now, before—"

"Amazing! Did you hear that, R'heet? Dense fog!"

"Incredible!"

"Ahem. What did history record as to the attainments of Technor Fourth Class S'lunt?"

"Yours was a dizzying career. I wonder, while you're at it, could you just make that Chicago? I've got a brother-in-law there. Well, not exactly a brother-in-law; actually he's the brother of a girl who was engaged to the fellow who later married my sister's husband's brother—but you know what I mean."

"I wonder if those hemlines ever went down again? I mean, for some girls it's all right, but if you don't happen to have a cute navel . . ."

"What about my General Minerals shares?" S'lunt inquired plaintively.

"They dropped to the ankle," Roger announced.

"Good Lord! But I assume they recovered and rose again? Probably higher than ever, eh?"

"Actually, they went even lower than that," Roger groped. "Of course, there was a corresponding adjustment at the top."

"Well, I should think so! That scoundrel F'hoot should never have been elected Chairman of the Board!"

"At the top? Wouldn't that be rather revealing?"

"In the end, the whole thing was exposed," Roger amplified desperately. "But about my going home . . ."

"Well, I'm glad to hear that F'hoot's chicanery was brought out in the open," S'lunt commented.

"I really shouldn't be thinking about fashions at a time like this, but I just can't help wondering what eventually happened to women's clothes."

"What about the rest of the Board?" S'lunt asked.

"Uh, they finally got rid of them entirely," Roger said, "but—"

"Goodness!"

"You don't mean . . . they did away with the whole capitalistic system?" R'heet exclaimed.

"It was a good thing, actually." Roger attempted to justify the implication. "It put an end to all that speculating."

"Gracious! I'm glad I never lived to see it!"

"Hrumph! Well, I hope it doesn't happen in my time!" a man in blue put in.

"Actually, it'll be along in the very near future, so how about turning me loose and concentrating your attention on your investments?"

"It appears I'll be stripped of my holdings entirely!" S'lunt predicted.

"History records that everyone was allowed to keep the bare essentials."

"B-but—what about when it got cold?"

"It's an outrage! I'm to be beggared—at my time of life?"

"With your reputation, I'm sure you'll find a partner with money," Roger suggested. "He'll probably have some way-out ideas to try, too."

"Why, of all the impertinent suggestions!"

"I'm too old," S'lunt mourned. "Too old to start again."

"You don't want to just sit on the sidelines and watch, do you, while the others have all the fun?"

"No . . . I suppose not," S'lunt sighed. "But it is rather depressing news."

"It sounds like an orgy!"

"It's not that bad," Roger said. "Just a mild depression. Afterwards things really got exciting—"

"*It's outrageous! The whole world running around stark naked!*"

"Who said anything about being stark naked?" Roger demanded.

There was a sharp gasp from the periphery of Roger's fascinated audience. A slim black-haired figure, exuberantly female in white skin-tights, thrust to the fore, pointed a finger at Roger.

"Put the disorganizer beam back on him, quick!" she cried. "He's a spy! He's been reading my mind!"

Roger came to his feet with a leap, staring at the newcomer. "Y-y-y-you!" he stuttered.

It was the girl he had left for dead beside the crashed motorcycle.

CHAPTER SIX

1

"I'm no spy!" Roger shouted over the hubbub that greeted the girl's dramatic charge. "I was just an ordinary citizen, going about my business, until *she* came along!"

"I've never seen this person before in my life," his accuser stated coldly.

"You gave me the message!" Roger countered. "You said it was of vast importance, and that—"

"What message?" she demanded.

"The one you gave me after you were dead! You made me steal that vegetable's motorcycle and go into the men's room!"

"He's raving," Q'nell said. "S'lunt, you'd better disassociate him at once! I'm sure he's part of some sort of plot to abort our probe!"

"Just a moment," S'lunt said. "What was that about a message?"

"S'lunt! Technor S'lunt? It was addressed to you!" Roger blurted. "I remember now!"

"What was the substance of this message?"

"She said she'd been, ah, partially successful, that was it!"

"Yes—go on?"

"I, ah, don't exactly remember the rest, but . . ."

"How unfortunate," S'lunt said grimly. "Just where is it you claim to have met Q'nell?"

"A few miles outside of the town of Mongoose, Ohio! In a rainstorm! At one o'clock in the morning!"

"Highly circumstantial," Q'nell conceded. "However, inasmuch as I have never been near Mongoose, Ohio, particularly in a rainstorm, your story doesn't hold up."

"There was an accident!" Roger insisted. "You, er, fell off your machine, and I rushed forward to render aid!"

"How selfless of you," the girl replied icily. "However—"

"That was when you told me to take that little gold button and put it in my ear!"

A shocked silence greeted this remark. Q'nell put a hand up, touched her ear.

"Why, he's talking about the Reinforcer," S'lunt said.

"Look!" R'heet pointed. All eyes went to Roger's ear. He angled his head to give them a better view.

"You see?" he said. "There it is, just like I said!"

"That's impossible," a man in mauve gasped. "There is only one Reinforcer, as we know only too well!"

"And I'm wearing it!" Q'nell stated emphatically.

"No you're not!" Roger contradicted. "I took it, just like you told me to, and—"

"Look!" She turned her head. The gold button gleamed dully in her ear.

"I wonder!" S'lunt said suddenly. "Q'nell—you say the fellow was reading your mind?"

Q'nell nodded curtly.

"There is one possible explanation. . . ." S'lunt looked thoughtfully at Roger. "What is she thinking at this moment?"

"Ah . . . she's thinking I'd be kind of cute if my nose wasn't so big. . . ." He broke off to finger his nose and dart a resentful glance at the girl.

"Q'nell, can you detect his thoughts?"

"Why . . . I don't know. . . ." She cocked her head as if listening. She gasped. "Well, of all the fresh things!"

"You hear him?"

"I heard *someone!*"

"It was me," Roger confirmed smugly.

"S'lunt, you were about to offer an explanation," R'heet reminded him.

"Yes. It's a bit fantastic, but then what isn't these days? We're preparing to launch our probe in exactly thirty-three minutes. Suppose we do so—and that the attempt is partially successful, as this chap stated Q'nell had reported. That would imply that rather than tracing the Channel to its origin, the mission was aborted at some point short thereof—possibly in the locality of Mongoose, Ohio. If Q'nell then encountered this person—"

"Tyson. Roger Tyson."

"You mean—she's already gone?" R'heet looked puzzled.

"Not yet. Still, in the future she will have gone, and if subsequently a message regarding her attempt were transmitted back here to us, via this rather unlikely messenger—"

"Tyson's the name. Roger—"

"But—she was to be dispatched in a retrogressive direction! Thus, if she did drop out of the Channel along the way, it would have been in the past—and this man comes from the future, as demonstrated by his encyclopedic grasp of upcoming developments!

"Perhaps our assumptions regarding the orientation of the manifold were in error; but that's a detail we can work out later. At the moment, the question is: What was the substance of the message which Q'nell will send back?"

"Look here, fellow—" R'heet started.

"Tyson," Roger supplied. "I'm sorry about the message. It was something about rocks, I remember that."

"Well, I suppose we might as well deploy the mind-stripper again," R'heet said ominously.

"Hold it! I just remembered something else. Something about sending a, ah, null-engine to . . . to the terminal to, er, break something or other!"

"A null-engine? But that would be a measure of desperation!" R'heet muttered.

"Still, it hangs together," S'lunt pointed out. "Your mission, Q'nell, was to determine the nature of the Entity, and attempt to deal with it. Failing that, alternatives were to be explored.

"And it seems the former approach failed. Leaving us no choice but to plunge all the way to the terminal coordinates and shatter the time lock utterly!"

"Ummmm. That being the case, we'd best extract what we can from this fellow—"

"Tyson. Roger Tyson."

"—and get on with it."

"Wait!" Q'nell said sharply. "If what you're saying is correct—then his story is also true! He must have come to my assistance and then undertaken to deliver my message just out of sheer altruism! Are we to reward him by boiling his brain and leaving him a babbling idiot?"

"Hmmm. Seems a little ungrateful," S'lunt conceded. "Still—we need to know all we can before you go."

"You mean you're still sending her on this mission—knowing she'll be killed?" Roger charged. "Why don't you just let me and all your other victims out of our cages and call the whole operation off!"

"I'm afraid you have an erroneous grasp of matters," S'lunt said in the surprised silence that greeted this proposal. "We're as much prisoners of the Museum as you seem to be. And unless we can solve the mystery of its construction—soon—we will all remain trapped here, for all eternity!"

2

"When we first discovered ourselves to be entoiled in a trap," S'lunt explained, leading the way out onto an unrailed terrace jutting over an orderly landscape half a mile below, "we of Culture One refused to panic. The enclave, happily, included the laboratory complex you see about you. We at once set to work to establish the parameters of our situation."

Roger held back as the others started across a yard-wide walkway arching over empty space to the adjoining structure. S'lunt gave him an interrogatory glance. "Why are you crouching in that fashion, sir?"

"It's just a thing I've got about heights," Roger confided. "Suppose I just wait here."

"Nonsense. I insist you join us on the pinnacle for a cuppa."

"You go ahead, then. I'll follow in my own way."

"Our studies," S'lunt said, strolling slowly as Roger progressed on all fours at his side, "have not been entirely fruitless. We have made certain determinations regarding the nature of the spatio-temporal distortion. Using a special tracer beam to follow our explorers through the point of tangency through which it is possible to pass from one display to another, we have determined that a progressive degeneration of temporal binding forces is at work, allowing artifacts and fauna of each era to wander into anachronistic settings, thus engendering massive energy imbalances which must end in disaster! On the basis of those findings, we designed and constructed the Reinforcer. With the aid of this device, the selected agent would, we hoped, be enabled to pass not only transversely across the Museum, but longitudinally along the Axial Channel as well, thus tracing the phenomenon to its source, and, hopefully, discovering the identity of the power behind it.

"How do you know it's a museum?" Roger inquired. He opened one eye and quickly closed it again.

"An assumption. The displays present a panorama of Terrestrial history from the dawn of life to its eventual sublimation."

"Then—why not just find another, ah, display, from the distant future where they have even more advanced science than you folks here in Culture One and—"

"Impossible. In the first place, the displays number ten billion, four hundred and four million, nine hundred and forty-one thousand, six hundred and two. Thus, investigating them at the rate of one per minute, the time required—"

"I get the idea," Roger interrupted. "What's the second place?"

"It would be the merest chance if we happened on a center of population or a scientific installation which would afford the necessary hardware, even if we succeeded in pinpointing a suitably advanced culture. So we have devoted the available time and manpower to the probe scheme."

"Say, that reminds me . . ." Roger said as he rose to his feet on the far side, where tables were placed under gay-colored umbrellas. "Some friends of mine were about to be eaten by a bear. How about just fetching them along here the way you did me?"

"Impossible. In your case, we were able to trace your movements via the emanations of the Reinforcer—though we didn't understand the nature of the signal at the time. But I'm afraid there's nothing we can do about the others. However, don't fret. They'll be right as rain after Turnover."

"Another thing I just remembered: I had some, uh, baggage with me . . ."

"Lost, I'm afraid. You must have dropped it when we put the grappler on you. Don't fret, however, I can lend you whatever you need."

"See here, Tyson," R'heet steered the conversation back to the problem at hand. "You might be a big help to us, having wandered through a number of the displays. Why don't you just let us strip down your brain a little—we'll leave you with the ability to feed yourself and possibly even tie your own shoelaces—"

"You can't!" Q'nell said promptly.

"Q'nell, your scruples are interfering with the orderly exploration of the facts," R'heet complained. "If I'd realized you were so emotional, I'd never have offered to sign a cohabitation agreement with you!"

"No need to upset yourself," Q'nell said coolly. "It has nothing to do with emotion. But have you stopped to think that his brain is linked to mine by an identical Reinforcer? You see the obvious corollary, I assume."

"Hmmm. If we squeeze his brain, the harmonics will destroy your mind as well."

"Too bad, fellows," Roger said. "Much as I'd like to help you out, I can't see letting the little lady suffer."

"I don't suppose we could remove the Reinforcer?" a man in puce vestments said doubtfully.

"You know better than that, D'olt. The filamentary system is inextricably intermingled with T'son's neural circuitry. Tampering with it would instantly prove fatal, as it did when T'son here removed it from Q'nell."

"You mean—I killed her?" Tyson blurted. "Good night, Miss Q'nell—excuse me!"

"It's nothing. If I ordered you to do so, I doubtless had my reasons."

"You're certainly being a sport about it," Roger said admiringly.

"We citizens of Culture One seldom descend to the level of purely emotional reactions," the girl stated calmly.

"Oh, really?" Roger raised an eyebrow. "I seem to recall seeing you blush just a few minutes ago."

"My physiological reactions system bears no relationship to my intellectually determined course of action," Q'nell snapped.

"Ah-ah! Anger, anger!" Roger said playfully. "Actually you're not a bad-looking girl at all, you know. Why don't you and I—"

"May I remind you, T'son," R'heet put in, "that I have offered Q'nell a cohabitation contract. Your attentions are therefore unwelcome."

"Well, let's just see what she says about that. . . ."

"I say that it's only twelve minutes until jump-off," Q'nell said flatly. "I'd better be getting into position."

"Don't let her do it! She'll be killed!" Roger protested.

"Possibly not," R'heet said calmly. "The change in the nature of her mission from exploratory probe to a bombing run introduces a new factor into the equation."

"You're a cold-blooded one!" Roger said. "At least delay the launch! Give me time to try to remember the rest of what she said!"

"No delay is possible," S'lunt put in. "The cyclical nature of the phenomenon requires that the attempt be within six hours, or never—at least not for another hundred and twelve years, by which time the deterioration of the temporal matrix will have progressed to the point where the entire space-time continuum will collapse on itself, with disastrous results!"

"Then wait six hours! There's no use going before the last second!"

"Turnover is in fifteen minutes. At that time, of course, the Reinforcer, if still in this temporal matrix, will revert to its constituent parts. Thus, let us make haste."

"But—but you can't send a girl like that out alone with a bomb!"

S'lunt made a burping sound at R'heet, who belched a reply. S'lunt turned to Roger with outstretched hand.

"Capital!" he said. "R'heet and I have discussed the matter in depth, and we agree there's no reason to refuse your courageous offer!"

"What offer?"

"To accompany her, of course! Let's hurry along, now! There's just time to pump the canned hypnobriefing into you before you go!"

3

"Comfort yourself, T'son," S'lunt said in a tone of easy assurance as he and the half dozen other launch technicians studied their instrument readings. "The perceptor circuits indicate that you have correctly absorbed your briefing and are now as aware as necessary of the parameters within which you will function. Everything is in readiness for your departure. Q'nell has the null-engine tucked away in her pocket, armed and ready. No point in waiting."

Glumly, Roger allowed himself to be escorted across the wide milk-glass floor to the spot where Q'nell waited beside a vast coil of thick white-painted tubing. R'heet emitted a terse *blap!* as he came up.

"I don't savvy the local Speedspeak," Roger said, noting the girl's pert features, short-clipped jet-black hair, and appealingly pink lips, slightly parted to show perfect teeth. "What was that all about?"

Q'nell gave him a glance which had receded several degrees toward the impersonal.

"He was just mentioning that your fear index was rising steadily. If it ascends another point or two, you'll be rigid with terror."

"Oh, I will, will I?" Roger said hotly. "Well, go check your dials, buster! Sure, I'm a little nervous! Who wouldn't be? For all I know, when I step into that thing I may wind up on an ice floe with a polar bear—or in the midst of a dinosaur's lunch—or swimming in the middle of the Indian Ocean—or—" His voice rose higher as a succession of images presented themselves, none of them pleasant.

"Oh, no danger of that," S'lunt said encouragingly. "Once launched along the Channel proper, you'll be outside the Museum entirely, moving in a physical context regarding the exact nature of which we can make only the vaguest conjectures."

"I remember you saying something like that, but I didn't know what it meant," Roger said. "By the way, what *does* it mean?"

"It moans," the girl put in, "that if your control should fail, we'll be ejected from the Channel into a nonspatial context."

"I've been thinking it over," Roger said promptly, "and I've decided this is too dangerous for a girl. Too bad; we might have solved everything—and of course I'd have loved going—but it means risking the life of a fragile little creature like you—"

"You're right, R'heet," Q'nell said, nodding. "I can sense the terror from here."

"Terror?" Roger came back hotly. "I was just . . ." He swallowed. "Scared," he finished. "But I've been scared before, and it never did me any good." He straightened his back. "Let's get going before I examine that statement too closely." He gripped the girl's head and advanced to the opening in the coil. As he stepped through, the familiar gray mist folded in about him.

"Now—we pause here!" Q'nell said. "Remember S'lunt's instructions!"

Roger closed his eyes and attempted to rotate his self-concept ninety degrees. Imagining his eyes to be peering out from the approximate position of his right ear was a difficult trick; a lifetime of orientation toward an arbitrarily designated "front" was not easy to overcome. But after all, he reminded himself, there was no reason the mind, an intangible field produced by the flow of current in a neural circuit, should be bound by such mundane restrictions. . . .

Suddenly he succeeded, was aware of the nose on the side of his head, of the sideburn growing down between his imaginary eyes, of his arms, one on the front, one on the back . . .

And then he was falling through some medium that was not space. . . .

CHAPTER SEVEN

1

For a while Roger fell with his eyes screwed shut, gripping the warm little hand of his partner—the sole material object in the universe. She appeared, he noted, to be about the size of the *Queen Mary*, floating majestically a mile away, linked to him by a fantastically long arm which dwindled as it approached, joining with a hand of normal size. Then he realized he had been mistaken. She was actually miscroscopically small, and floated on the surface of his eyeball. . . .

"Not too bad so far," she said. There were no audible words; the thought formed in Roger's mind with crystal clarity, in the girl's voice, complete with overtones of a passionate nature rigidly concealed beneath a calm exterior.

"How did you do that?" Roger inquired, and noted with surprise that his lips failed to move. Neither was he breathing. In sudden alarm, he tried to draw in air, but nothing happened.

"Don't struggle," Q'nell's mental voice spoke

sharply. "We're in a null-time state, where events like heartbeats and respiration can't take place. Don't let it distract you, or we'll find ourselves expelled from the Channel."

"How long is this going to take?" Roger asked nervously. He felt no physical distress from lack of air, but a conviction of suffocation was rising in him.

"No time at all—other than subjectively," Q'nell said.

"How can we be sure we're actually going anywhere? Maybe we're just going to hang here in space forever, swelling and shrinking."

"That's just your parameters trying to adjust to the absence of physical stimuli," Q'nell pointed out. "Don't let it bother you. And stop asking questions. If we knew the answers, we wouldn't be here."

"Hey!" Roger said suddenly. "My eyes are still shut; I can feel them! How is it I can see you?"

"You are not seeing me, you're apprehending me directly."

"This gray stuff," Roger said. "It's just like what you always see when you close your eyes. You know, I'm beginning to wonder—"

"Don't!" Q'nell said sharply. "Whatever you do, don't start to wonder!"

"I can't help it!" Roger retorted. "This is all too ridiculous to be true! Any second now I'm going to wake up—in my own bed, back in Elm Bluffs, with my mother calling me," he added, prompted by a sudden, vivid sense of homesickness.

The gray mist was changing, forming up into walls that simultaneously receded and closed in on him. Splotches appeared, congealed into large, pastel-colored floral patterns. There was a tear in the wallpaper, with white plaster showing behind it. He sat up, stared dumbly around a big, airy room with a ceiling that slanted down at one side, open windows, a shelf stacked with dog-eared Tom Swift books and untrimmed pulp magazines with B. Paul covers. Several inaccurately aligned model planes dangled from the ceiling on strings; a framed butterfly collection hung on the wall beside a row of arrowheads wired to a board and a felt pennant lettered ELM BLUFFS SR. HIGH.

"Roger!" a voice called in an unmistakably maternal tone. "If I have to call you again . . . " The unuttered threat hung in the air.

Roger made a squeaking sound, staring down at his own body. He saw a narrow, ribby chest, rumpled pajama bottoms covering knobby knees, the spindly shanks of a thirteen-year-old boy. "But . . . but . . ." he mumbled. "I'm thirty-one years old, and a grown-up failure! I was in the Channel with Q'nell, headed for the terminal coordinates. . . ." He paused, frowning. "Terminal what?" he said aloud. "Wow, did I dream some big words!"

Suddenly the room faded, the walls swirled away into formless mist. Q'nell's face appeared, floating toward him.

"Where did you go?" she demanded. "You disappeared!"

"I was a boy again," Roger stuttered. "I was back home, in my own bed. It was just as real as this—realer! I could feel the bed under me, and smell bacon cooking, and feel the breeze coming through the window! I thought all *this* was a dream!"

"But—you couldn't. It's impossible! *I'm* the dominant member of this linkage! You can't do anything I don't order you to do! At least that's the theory. . . ."

"That's ridiculous," Roger said. "You're only a girl, remember?"

"Look here, T'son! Don't go wrecking the mission with your irresponsible male chauvinism! For some reason—probably having to do with a temporal precession effect induced by the reduplication of the Reinforcer circuitry—you seem to have taken over control of our joint conceptualizing capacities. You'll have to exercise extreme care not to do anything impulsive! Unless we keep all our faculties attuned to the mission, you and I and a few million other captives will spend the rest of Eternity reliving the same day—or worse!"

A faint nebulosity had appeared nearby, at the edge of Roger's vision. It grew, took on form and color.

"Q'nell!" Roger shouted soundlessly. "Look!"

"Now, T'son, if you're going to go on panicking every twenty-one subjective seconds, our mission is doomed. Try to relax."

"Behind you!" He stared at the knotted blanket slowly drifting into view. Under the brown folds, something was stirring, like a cat in a croker-sack.

"It's revived!" Roger blurted. "The monster!"

"Now, T'son, you know we studied your statements back in Culture One and decided that the monster concept was merely a subconscious projection—"

"Projection or not, we've got to get out!" Roger gritted his mental teeth, concentrating on the image of the homey bedroom, the flowered wallpaper. . . .

A vague pathway seemed to open through the surrounding gray. Roger yearned toward it, felt himself slipping into it. . . .

"T'son! What are you doing?" Q'nell's mental voice had assumed an odd, echoing quality. The tunnel was closing in, condensing into deep gloom that bulked around Roger. Sharp things poked at his back; the smell of hay was thick in his nostrils. He was, he saw, lying in a stack of the stuff, itching furiously. Overhead the lofty ceiling of a barn loomed.

"Now you've done it!" a familiar voice sounded, somewhere to the rear of his left eye. *"I warned you about this sort of thing!"*

"Where are we?" Roger sat up, scratched at a center of irritation on his right elbow, another on the left side of his neck, reached for a spot on his shoulder.

"Get the one on our left knee," Q'nell commanded. *"Then get us out of here!"*

"My God!" Roger mumbled. "Are you in the same skin with me?"

"Where else would I be, you dolt?" Q'nell retorted. *"We're linked; where you go, I go, unfortunately for me. S'lunt was mad to entrust this mission to you! I might have known you'd panic and spoil it all!"*

"Who's panicked! And you can scratch your own knee!" Promptly his left arm, as if possessed of a vitality all its own, did just that. Startled, Roger rose to his feet, and promptly fell on his face, since his left leg had failed to join in the effort to support him.

"I'll take the left half," Q'nell's voice stated firmly. *"You'll take the right. Now reattune and get us back into the Channel!"*

Roger tried to protest, but the left half of his face was wooden. "I'm paralyzed," he yelped incoherently. Threshing, he rolled from the hay onto a packed dirt floor. Across the room a wide door swung open. A tall, lean man in overalls, pitchfork in hand, stood outlined against a pale early-morning sky.

"Aha, it's you, is it, Andy Butts!" an irate voice grated. "I told you for the last time about sneaking into my barn and upsetting George and Elsie! By hokey, you'll work off your night's lodging! You can start by forking out those stalls! Now come out of there and set to!"

Roger struggled to balance himself on all fours, but fell on his face instead.

"Drunk, too!" the man wth the pitchfork barked, advancing with the weapon poised. "You'd better sober up in one gosh-blasted hurry, or by Jupiter I'll give you a taste of what the hereafter'll be like! Get up!" He jabbed with the gleaming tines. Roger made inarticulate sounds and scrabbled one-armed and one-legged, describing a circle in the dust. The owner of the barn stared at him blankly.

"Goldang, Andy!" he blurted. "You all right?"

"Help!" Roger shouted. The sound emerged as a gargle. He fell on his face again.

"Andy! You've had a stroke!" the pitchforker yelled, tossing the implement aside. "Rest easy, Andy! I'll go for Doc Whackerby!"

With a supreme effort, Roger assumed sufficient control to cause the body of Andy Butts to spring wildly to its feet and topple, arms windmilling, against the barn owner, sending him spinning before crashing, jaw first, to the ground.

"He's went insane!" the man yelled, staggering to his feet. He dashed away shouting.

"What are you trying to do?" Q'nell demanded subvocally. *"That maniac almost murdered us!"*

"Give me back my leg!" Roger countered. "We've got to get out of here!"

"Transfer us back to the Channel!" Q'nell commanded. *"Until you do, I'm not letting go!"*

"Are you crazy? You'll feel that pitchfork just as much as I will!"

"Oh, no I won't! I'm leaving the sensory nervous system entirely to you, thanks!"

"But I don't know how!" Roger yelled silently.
"Try!"

"Well . . ." Lying on the floor, Roger closed his eye. He stared into the formless gray, swimming with pulsating points and lines of pale-colored light, searching for some clue—any clue to escape. Instead, he was aware of the weight of fat on the body he now occupied, the rasp of stubble on his jowls, the pains shooting from his empty stomach, a clammy, shivering feeling of early-morning hangover.

"Ugh!" Q'nell exclaimed. *"How revolting!"*

"Quiet! How can I concentrate!"

"Hurry up! That barbarian's coming back!"

"I'm trying!" Roger gritted his teeth, realized with a dull shock that he was grinding toothless gums together, became aware simultaneously of the coating on his tongue, a gluey feeling about the eyes, small creatures exploring his scalp, dirty socks—and an unreasoning dread of Doc Whacker-by.

"He's trying to take over!" Roger shouted soundlessly. "The owner of this miserable body!" With an effort, he forced his attention away from the reactions of Andy Butts, blanking his mind to allow his hypnotic training to come to the fore. The grayness thinned, receding. Two foci of relative brightness swam into his ken, radiating calmness.

"I think I've located our bodies!" he communicated. "I'll try to bring them in. . . ." He willed himself toward the objectives, which floated, vague and formless, in the remote distance—or millimeters away. He was faintly aware of excited voices approaching, of pounding feet, of a renewed pang of Buttsian fear. With a final desperate effort, he lunged mentally for the nearest brightness, felt a wrench as Q'nell was torn from his side—

He was in a tiny space that compressed him like a straitjacket. Sounds crackled and boomed around him; sharp odors assailed his nostrils. Blurry gray and white forms moved vaguely before him. He tried to move, to call out, felt the shift of cumbersome members, the play of remote, impersonal muscles stretching under insensitive hide. His field of view swung, came to rest on a massive bulk beside him. He blinked, made out the shape of a vast draft horse in the next stall.

"Q'nell!" he tried to shout, instead uttered a bleating whinny. He recoiled, felt an obstruction behind him. At once, in instinctive reaction, his rear legs shot out in a frantic kick. Boards shattered and split. A surge of equine panic sent him blundering through the side of the stall.

Small, excited figures scattered before him. He longed for open space, charged toward it, burst into the open, shied as something tall and dark loomed before him, leaped a fence, and galloped for the safety of the open plains. . . .

A detailless image of the comforting bulk of the mare rose in his mind. He slowed, rounded into the wind, sniffed for her distinctive scent. He felt his heart pounding slowly, massively, was aware of air snorting in through wide nostrils, felt himself quivering with a fear that drained away as memory of its origin faded from his mind. He tossed his head and trotted back toward the barn. The mare appeared, galloping into perfect focus. She came up to him, nuzzled him—

"T'son! What have you done?"

The words seemed to mean something—almost. But the effort to unravel the meaning was too much. . . .

"T'son! Use your training! Pull yourself together! Remember the mission!"

He lunged playfully for the mare, followed as she retreated, inspired suddenly by a vague but powerful urge which impelled him to rear and whinny, renew the pursuit.

"Stop that, you idiot!" Q'nell commanded as he succeeded in shouldering alongside her. She retreated frustratingly. He lunged again.

"Try, T'son! You can do it! Concentrate. Align your parameters!"

"Elsie—you're beautiful!" Roger succeeded in formulating the thought into word-patterns. "So desirable! So . . . so horsy!"

"I'll horsy you if we ever get out of this one, you

cretin!" Q'nell's silent voice penetrated his euphoria. *"Remember the Channel? Remember the Museum, and all those people, locked up in it like capuchin monkeys? Remember how you were going to trace the system back to its source and become the savior of us all?"*

"Yes . . . I remember . . . sort of. But it all seems so unimportant, compared with that lovely, shapely, inviting—"

"Later, T'son!" Q'nell said frantically. *"First, you get us back where we belong; then we'll talk about my shapely inviting!"*

"I don't want to talk," Roger capered, pawing the turf. "I want action!"

"The Channel, T'son! Here comes the farmer! He'll hitch you up to a plow and work you like a horse all day, and tonight you'll be too tired to do anything at all!"

"I don't want to plow; I want to—"

"I know!" Q'nell sounded desperate. *"But back in the Channel we can be together!"*

"Together? In the channel?" Roger struggled to fix the concept in his cramped, dimly lit mind. He remembered the grayness, the presence that had drifted beside him there. And there it was now, hovering near at hand, a dim blur, and another beyond . . .

"No, T'son! That's the farmer and another man! Keep looking! Narrow your parameters!"

Roger groped outward, swimming upward. Or was it sideways? Or no, he was falling . . . falling endlessly through the medium that was not space, and there, linked to his outstretched hand was . . . was . . .

"You blundering imbecile!" Q'nell's voice came through loud and clear. "You've gotten us back inside the wrong bodies!"

2

"How could you ever have made such an idiotic mistake?" Q'nell queried for the thirty-fifth time in four minutes. "Trapping me inside your clumsy, undisciplined, *masculine* corpus!"

"Well, I'm just as badly off, aren't I?" Roger replied. "I'm stuck in this silly, flimsy female body of yours!" He felt an unaccountable impulse to cry—not that he felt any particularly poignant emotion; it just seemed like the thing to do. "I was only trying to do what you said!"

"Ha! If I'd only sided with R'heet and gone ahead and dug the Reinforcer out of your skull by force, instead of going all mushy inside and voting to keep you alive."

"What? You mean that two-faced sneaky little R'heet suggested that? Why, I'll scratch his eyes out—I mean, I'll knock his block off," Roger corrected.

"Don't start wandering again!" Q'nell warned sharply. "You're just barely holding us in stasis now! We can't afford to drop out again!"

"It could have happened to anybody," Roger said loftily. "Now, please don't bother me with your petty little complaints unless you have something constructive to contribute."

"Constructive! If it hadn't been for me, you'd still have been horsing around, trying to—"

"Please!" At the recollection of his recent emotions, Roger felt what would have been a deep-purple blush if his blood had been circulating. "Suppose we discuss what we're going to do when we get there," he hurried on. "Now, my idea is that we just go right up to whoever's in charge and give them a piece of our mind."

"Don't try to think, T'son!" Q'nell boomed. "Leave that to me. Your job is just to keep us focused while I do the actual work. As for what we do when we get there, inasmuch as we haven't the faintest idea what we'll find, suppose we play it by ear, eh? You just take your cue from me."

"Well! What makes you so superior?" Roger came back.

"Say!" Q'nell cut in. "It just dawned on me! If I've got your body, I've also got your limited brain!"

"Don't you dare use my brain!" Roger ordered sharply.

"Quiet; I'm checking out the circuitry," Q'nell ordered. "If I'm stuck with it, I may as well see what I have to work with. . . ." There was a momentary pause. "Say—you've got a lot of unused capacity here! I might be able to use it!"

"You just stick to our orders," Roger insisted. "Now that I've gotten us back where we belong— well, practically back where we belong—don't go spoiling it all experimenting!"

"Orders are made to be broken," Q'nell said callously. "I've got a notion that if I just nudge this parameter *here*—and then twist this one over *here*—"

Roger felt the insubstantial frame of reference about him tilt suddenly, flip upside down. "Stop!" he cried. "You're doing it wrong!"

"Oops! Hold on tight; looks as if maybe I should have twisted *that* one instead!"

There was a sickening sensation as space turned inside out. Roger felt himself expand instantaneously to infinite size, shrink as suddenly to minuteness, and disappear, to reemerge on the other side. Light burst in his face, sound roared. He was whirling, falling, sinking into cold syrup—

He fetched up with a thump, rolled over twice, and opened his eyes. He lay on an expanse of waving grasses which glowed eerily like an aquarium lit from below, under a sky of total velvety black. His body, he saw, shone in the dark, a soft, lightning-bug green. He looked across at the frightened-looking luminous man with rumpled hair who was sitting up nearby, rubbing an unshaven jaw.

My God, do I really have that bewildered look? He wondered, watching himself staring at the scenery.

"Well, don't lie there staring at me," Q'nell said over the roar and crackle of the sky. "Start having ideas!"

CHAPTER EIGHT

1

"Where do you suppose we are?" Roger inquired, gingerly brushing sparkling dust from the unaccustomed curves of his borrowed form.

"How do I know?" Q'nell snapped. She stamped awkwardly up and down like a spotlit performer, swinging Roger's arms and staring out across the shining landscape to a row of phosphorescent hills. "How the devil do you balance this infernal body? These feet weigh a ton—and the hip joints are too close together."

"Well! I'd trade back in a minute! I feel like my rear is a mile wide—and what do you do about the topheavy feeling?"

Q'nell glanced at him, then looked again, her gaze lingering. "Say, you know, that's not a bad-looking little form, if I do say so myself." She sauntered closer. "There's something kind of appealing about the way it sticks out here and there—and when it moves—" She broke off, a startled look on Roger's face. "Good heavens!"

she murmured. "Is *that* the way it feels to be a male?"

"Keep away from me, you onanist!" Roger shrilled, backing up, noting in passing that the sensation of alarm coursing through him had curiously pleasurable overtones.

"You poor thing," Q'nell said. "Imagine going around reacting like that to the mere sight of a female!"

"I'm no female! I'm Roger Tyson, one hundred percent red-blooded male man! And you keep your sticky hands to yourself! I mean, you keep *my* sticky hands to yourself!"

"Are you sure you want me to?" Q'nell advanced.

"Get back!" Roger yelped. "You're ogling again!"

"Well, why don't you cover yourself up, you—you exhibitionist! How do you expect me to keep my mind on the problem at hand with you undulating around? You're doing it on purpose! I suppose it gives you some kind of sense of power or something!"

"For the first time I'm getting an insight into the origin of Puritanism," Roger muttered. "It's dirty-minded voyeurs like you that are responsible for all the prudery in the world! It's not my fault if the sight of me upsets you!" He felt his—or Q'nell's—right hip execute a flawless grind, ending in a modest bump that set his superstructure quivering.

"Hey!" he yelped. "*I* didn't do that—it was this troublemaking body of yours! Suddenly I'm beginning to understand a lot of things about the battle of the sexes!"

"Why fight?" Q'nell inquired reasonably. Roger's face was twisted into an obnoxious smirk, he noted with dismay. Surely *he* had never looked at a helpless female that way!

"Hey!" Q'nell pointed past him. "Company coming!" She jumped forward to place herself before Roger as a weird spectacle appeared dramatically over a nearby ridge. It was a luminous horse of a pale, glowing turquoise shade, hung about with jet-black harness from which depended glittering baubles like Christmas-tree lights. Astride the creature's back sat a rider whose hide gleamed a pale blue. He was scantily garbed, topped by a nodding headdress of plumes like colored flames. The apparition galloped up to rein in facing the two adventurers at a distance of ten feet. The rider spoke, an effect like the blipping of blank spots on a magnetic tape.

"Take it easy, honey," Q'nell said grimly. "I'll handle this." She stepped forward, fists on hips, buzzed a speech in Culture One Speedspeak, at which the rider leaned from the saddle and fetched her a solid blow on the side of the head with a long knobbed stick.

"You monster!" Roger shrilled, springing forward to stand astride his fallen body.

"Wha—" Q'nell inquired, rolling groggily to Roger's feet. She leaped up suddenly, brushed Roger aside, caught the stick as it swung again, yanked the rider from the saddle. The mount shied and galloped away as the two rolled in the dust, blue arms and dusty white rising and falling to the accompaniment of dull thuds. Roger felt a curious thrill as Q'nell rolled clear and jumped up, dusting her borrowed hands.

"All right, who's next?" she yelled, waving Roger's fists. The blue man groaned.

"No takers," Q'nell said, smiling broadly. Roger had never before noticed what an inane smile he had . . . but on the other hand, it was rather cute in a way—almost boyish, as if he needed mothering.

"I've never understood before just what it was you fellows got out of all those body-contact sports," Q'nell said cheerfully. "But you know, there's something about crunching your knuckle into somebody's skull that's good for the repressed psyche!" She put a casual hand on Roger's shoulder. With horror, he felt his borrowed knees begin to quiver.

"Unhand me, you—you barbarian!" he squeaked, and threw the offending member off. "Just look at that poor man! You've hurt him!" He knelt by the fallen warrior, began dabbing ineffectually at the dust caking his face. The patient opened his eyes—a startling clear yellow, like illuminated lemon drops—and smiled, showing excellent teeth. The next second a blue hand was fumbling Roger's thigh. In instant reflex, he landed an open-handed slap across the reviving face that sent the blue casualty back for another count.

"Say, did that rapist try to get fresh?" Q'nell started, advancing pugnaciously.

"Never mind that," Roger countered. "Just get busy and get us out of here!"

"I've got a good mind to revive that degenerate and—"

"Q'nell! It was nothing! Now, let's concentrate on those parameters you were so worried about a few minutes ago!"

"Believe me, a maniac like that has just one thing in mind!"

"So have I: getting away from here! This is a totally alien environment, in case you haven't noticed! We're lucky we can even breathe the air! For all we know, we're soaking up a lethal dose of radiation right now!"

"I wonder"—Q'nell eyed the native with unabated hostility—"what gave the clown the idea . . ."

"You ought to know," Roger said. "All men are alike! I mean, the fact that he's a male— I mean, well, after all, it's perfectly natural, isn't it? I mean—"

"You led him on!" Q'nell charged. "Why, you promiscuous little tramp!"

"Q'nell! Come to your senses! Our lives are at stake! Thousands of lives! Now just figure out what you did before, and do it again, backwards."

"Actually, I've got a feeling we've flipped out into a reverse-polarity universe," Q'nell said carelessly. "But let's forget that for now. You know, T'son," she went on in an oily tone which made Roger's skin crawl, "you and I have never really had a chance to get acquainted." She edged closer. "Back in Culture One they kept me so busy dashing around I never really had time to notice what a charming, ah, personality you have."

"Skip my personality," Roger snapped. "Just get busy and retwiddle those parameters!"

"How'm I supposed to concentrate on all that technical business with this funny feeling creeping over me every time I look at that slinky little torso of yours, and that slender little waist, and those nice—"

"Look here, Q'nell!" Roger snapped, fending off his hands. "Get control of myself, girl! Put your intelligence in charge! Remember what S'lunt said! If this trap system isn't destroyed, it'll rip the whole space-time continuum wide open! Imagine the confusion, with Genghis Khan galloping around the middle of World War One, and Louis the Fifteenth coming face to face with de Gaulle, and Teddy Roosevelt bumping heads with LBJ, and—"

"All right, all right, you've made your point." Q'nell slumped back, breathing hard, promptly sat up again. "But are you sure you don't really want to—"

"No! Stick to the subject at hand! The Channel! It's not hard, Q'nell; just close your eyes and try to sort of firm up the gray into a nice even sort of custardy consistency."

"I'm trying," Q'nell said, squeezing Roger's eyes shut. "But it just looks like a lot of garbage to me."

Roger closed the eyes of the body he was occupying. "There's really nothing to it," he said in a calm, reasonable tone. "*I* didn't have any trouble. You just exclude all extraneous thoughts from your mind."

"Did you know that when you run you have the most delightful jounce?" Q'nell said.

"I assure you, it's unintentional!" Roger said icily. "Now concentrate! Think about it!"

"I am! I can't think about anything else! Great galloping galaxies, T'son, I really have to admire you men for the little restraint you show! It's like . . . like . . ."

"It's like nothing else in the world," Roger said. "I remember it well—even though it all seems pretty silly now, which goes to show the decisive role glands play in philosophy."

"I suppose you're right," Q'nell said resignedly. "But since it's really your fault for scrambling us up like this, you ought to be willing to—"

"Don't go feminine on me now!" Roger yelped. "We'll *both* concentrate! Maybe together we can manage it!" He groped mentally toward the insubstantial stuff floating before his closed eyes, but it boiled imperviously, stubbornly refusing to coalesce into the characteristic gray of the Channel.

"How are you doing, Q'nell?" he asked.

"I'm not sure . . . but I think . . . maybe . . ."

"Yes? Keep trying! You can do it!"

"Maybe," Q'nell went on, "you'd better open your eyes."

Roger complied instantly—and was looking up into the massed spears of a company of ghostly blue riders hemming them in from all sides.

2

"The very idea," Roger said an hour later, after a rough ride strapped behind a sweating blue warrior, and an unsatisfying interview in a pitch-dark room with unseen locals. "Putting us together in the same cell!"

"At least this way we only have one door to break down," Q'nell said. "What did you expect, separate suites? His and Hers buckets?"

"Must you be crude?" Roger folded his arms, quickly unfolded them, disconcerted by the sensation.

"Just realistic," Q'nell said. "Let's face facts: I'm

occupying an inferior brain. It's up to you, T'son. I did my best."

"What did you make of the interrogation?"

"What could I make of it? Total darkness, silent voices—I'm not even sure we were being questioned."

"Of course we were," Roger said loftily. "And they're not through yet. They'll be back soon."

"How do you know?"

"Feminine intuition."

"Oh, that!" Q'nell said disparagingly. "Just a mish-mash of wild guesses and wishful thinking."

"You'll see," Roger said complacently. "Now be quiet. Since you seem to be helpless, I'll have to try to do what I can." He stretched out on the floor and looked into the grayness swirling before his closed eyes . . .

. . . and was awakened by a foot prodding his side to see Q'nell struggling in the grip of a pair of husky fluorescent guards.

This time they were hustled unceremoniously along dull-glowing corridors out into a walled courtyard under an open sky just beginning to gray at zenith. Several dark points were visible there, like negative star images on an astronomical photograph.

"I think I'm beginning to understand what makes the light so funny," Roger confided to Q'nell as they stood together against one pockmarked wall. "The whole spectrum is shifted; we're seeing heat— that's why living things glow—and visible light is off in the radio range somewhere."

"I'm beginning to understand something even more fascinating than that," Q'nell said. "Those ten blue men over there with the guns in their hands are a firing squad!"

"You're a big success as a negotiator," Roger charged bitterly. "If this is a compromise, what were they holding out for?"

"At least we're not going to be tortured," Q'nell snapped back. "Be quiet and let's start concentrating! Maybe the spur of dire necessity will help me use some of the ninety-two percent of your brain our instruments showed was lying fallow!"

"I don't know how to operate your brain!"

"Well, try! It's a finely tuned instrument, trained in all the subtleties of Culture One mental science! Put it to use!"

Across the eerie courtyard, the rank of armed men were lining up, eyeing their prospective targets with shining yellow eyes. Roger shivered.

"I can't," he said. "All I can think about is what it will feel like to be shot!"

"In that case, I guess it's goodbye," Q'nell said. "I'm afraid your body's panic reactions are inhibiting my concentration, too."

"About those passes you were making," Roger said, feeling a sudden tenderness toward the girl. "I didn't mean to be stuffy or anything."

"Actually, I admire you for your stand," Q'nell said. "Only a tramp would have given in."

"What! Why, you practically fell all over yourself trying to make time with me! And if I'd taken pity on you, that makes me a tramp?"

"Calm down! I was complimenting you!"

"Of all the nerve! And I thought you liked me! And all the time you were just amusing yourself, testing my reactions!"

"Hey, that's not true! You're very appealing! I just meant that, uh . . . But what does it matter what I meant? This is the end. Goodbye, T'son. It's been very interesting."

Roger didn't answer. He was watching with fascination as the blue men loaded their guns. . . .

A vertical line of light quivered into existence between Roger and the aimed guns. It wavered, faded, firmed again, flickered. . . .

"T'son!" Q'nell said sharply. "It's a portal! It must be good old S'lunt!"

"He'd better hurry up and focus it," Roger said, gritting his teeth hard. "In about another two seconds—"

"On the count of three, hit the deck!" Q'nell hissed. "One!" The firing squad took aim.

"Two!"

The portal snapped into sharpness. A shape appeared, sliding forth from it—a bulbous shape, glowing a dull red, ringed about with jointed tentacles.

"Three!" Q'nell called. Roger dived flat, heard the close-spaced blips of silence that punctuated the background roar, saw the monster explode into a shower of fragments as it intercepted the fusillade intended for the humans. The shooters, astonished at the sudden obstacle that had interposed itself between them and their target, stood gaping dumbly as Roger and Q'nell came to their feet.

"Come on!" Q'nell yelled, and grapped Roger's hand.

"But—but it's one of *theirs!*" he protested, pulling back.

"Any port in a storm!" Q'nell shouted.

"I guess you're right," Roger gulped, and together they dashed forward and plunged through the portal.

CHAPTER NINE

1

They spun outward in a swirl of silence and light. Light foamed about them, glaring, sputtering, pulsing red and green and blue and gold, like a breaking comber of jewels.

"It's beautiful!" Q'nell's voice sounded in his head. "But what is it? We're not in the Channel. Our extrapolated universe model never predicted anything like this!"

"Nevertheless, it's here," Roger said. "And we're still alive to enjoy it."

"We've got to find out where we are and where we're going, in a hurry! We may be sliding right into their home base!"

"Yes. We seem to be traveling pretty fast," Roger agreed. As in the Channel, the sensation was of motion not through space, but through some subtler medium.

"I'm going to give the parameters another try," Q'nell said. "Somehow they seem to be much more accessible when we're in a non-space environment."

"Just don't go twisting them," Roger cautioned.

"That's precisely what I intend to do!" Q'nell countered. "But I'm afraid it will take more than a twist to get us back where we belong."

The clouds of light were changing, receding, forming up into towering thunderheads that glowed with pale colors. Now it was as though they swam in a stormy sky amid heaped, multicolored cumuli, with no up, no down, no land in sight. They swooped like effortless gulls between towers and through canyons, hurtling past vast, billowing domes, diving through airy tunnels, skimming the surface of cloudy plains.

"It's no good; I'm getting dizzy," Q'nell called at last. She was swooping in the middle distance, upside down. "There's no frame of reference whatever!"

"If we just had something underfoot," Roger said. "I'm afraid I'm going to be airsick!" As he spoke, he felt something nudge the soles of his shoes. He looked down, saw a patch of pale blue tiled floor.

"Q'nell! Look!" He waved to her, floating overhead now.

"Where did that come from?" she called.

"I just thought of it—and here it was!"

Q'nell swung closer, arced downward to thump lightly against the floor. "Say, T'son, you may be on to something here!" She poked at the floor with a finger, pounded with her fist. "It feels solid enough. This is amazing! We seem to be in a malleable continuum, which can be concretized by thought impulses!"

Roger went to hands and knees, crawled to the edge, reached under, and felt around.

"It's about an inch thick," he said. "Rough on the underside."

"Careful now, T'son," Q'nell cautioned. "Don't do anything that might shift our parameters, but . . . do you think you could extend it any?"

"I'll try. . . ." Roger closed his eyes, imagined the floor extending outward twenty feet on every side, ending in a smooth edge.

"You did it!" Q'nell said excitedly. "Good boy!" Opening his eyes, Roger was delighted to find the floor exactly as he had imagined it. They walked to the edge.

"You know, this is a little vertiginous, looking down at all that open air," Q'nell said, edging back. "How about filling it in a little?"

Roger pictured green grass under spreading shade trees.

"Remarkable!" Q'nell exclaimed, surveying the parklike result. "Suppose I have a try?"

"Careful," Roger said. "Just anyone may not have the brainpower to do it."

"Stand back," Q'nell said. As Roger watched, a wall winked into existence before his face. For a second or two it was plain white plaster; then a slightly crooked window with a purple-and-pink curtain was suddenly there, with sunlight streaming through it. Roger turned. He was in a room, walled, roofed—and carpeted a moment later in a pattern of pink and yellow flowers.

"Nothing to it," Q'nell said. "Now, a couple of chairs . . ." Two massive mismatched rockers appeared, complete with glossy black satin cushions lettered SAIGON and MOTHER in glowing blue.

"Horrible," Roger said. "Have you no taste?"

He pictured a pair of delicate Chippendales, added a side table with a silver tray bearing a steaming teapot and a pair of dainty cups. He seated himself.

"I'll pour," he offered.

"I'll take a drink of something with some vitamins in it!" Q'nell snorted, and a bottle with a garish label thumped to the table. She produced a corkscrew next, poured out a stiff cupful.

"Hey, that's good stuff!" she exclaimed, smacking loudly. "Want a snort?"

Roger caught a whiff of the powerful brew and shuddered. "Certainly not."

Q'nell poured herself a second, strolled around the room, adding garish pictures in gold frames to the wall, placing lamps with grotesque shades here and there while Roger winced.

"Not bad," she said. "But it still lacks something. . . ." She stared at a wall; a door appeared. She opened it on a bedroom containing nothing but an enormous bed.

"How about it, T'son?" she leered. "Feeling tired?"

"Now don't start all that again," Roger said. "The only purpose of this house-building spree was to help us with our orientation, remember?"

"All work and no play make Jackie a dull girl," Q'nell said.

"You've already given me your opinion of playgirls!" Roger yelled. "And anyway, I'm a man! Now stop horsing around and give your attention to the problem!"

"I am, T'son—I am!" Q'nell poured a third hearty libation, drank it, put the cup down, and reached for Roger. He leaped up and dodged behind a rocker.

"Stop it or I'll imagine the biggest policeman you ever heard of!" he yelled.

"Oh yeah?" Q'nell made a grab, missed, almost fell. "Say, that booze is getting to me," she murmured. "Oh, well, it helps the party atmosphere." She tossed the cup aside and lunged, hooked a foot on the rocker, and landed headfirst.

"I warned you!" Roger closed his eyes and pictured a seven-foot storm trooper, complete with spurred boots, brass knuckles, and a knotted leather whip. There was a soft *thud!* and a metallic tinkle. He opened his eyes to see an empty uniform collapse to the floor.

Q'nell leaped to her feet. "I didn't think you'd have the heart!" she cried blurrily, starting around the chair. Roger pictured a stairway, dashed for it, went up the steps two at a time, found himself on a landing open to the sky. Feet pounded below.

"More stairs!" he commanded, and dashed on. It was a glass-and-chrome-rail construction, rising in a gentle spiral. Too bad he hadn't called for an elevator; he was getting winded.

"Roof!" Q'nell shouted behind him. The sky was blotted out as a solid ceiling appeared above him, supported by sturdy walls.

"Door!" Roger countered, jerking open the panel which had instantly winked into existence, and was on a wide, featureless roof. He whirled, slammed the door.

"Yale lock!" he gasped, out of breath. He turned the shiny brass key and leaned against the door, panting.

"Fooled you!" Q'nell called, clambering over the parapet. "Fire escape!"

"Rope ladder!" Roger demanded, sprang for the dangling rungs, and clambered rapidly upward. Overhead, the vast translucent bulk of a balloon swayed, the words OMAHA, NEBRASKA spelled out in yard-high letters across its bulbous side.

"Bow and arrow!" Q'nell's voice floated up from below. An instant later there was a sharp twang, the swish of the bolt in flight, a ripping noise, succeeded by a loud hissing. The balloon began to sink rapidly. Moments later Roger slammed against the roof and was immediately engulfed in the deflated folds of the balloon. He fought his way clear, scrambled up, looked wildly around for Q'nell.

His companion lay sprawled by the parapet, unconscious. Beside the body, a monster, dull red, one-eyed, squatted on clustered legs, a figure of infinite menace.

"Machine gun!" Roger yelled, felt the solid slap of the weapon into his hands. He jacked the action, swung it to bear on the alien—

A dazzling light glared in his eyes. He felt the gun fall from his hands, felt his knees begin to buckle; then a Roman candle exploded inside his skull and scattered his consciousness in bright fragments that faded and were lost in darkness.

2

Roger came to himself lying on a hard floor. He pried his eyes open and sat up—and instantly grabbed for support. He was perched, he saw, on a tiny platform dangling by a single thin wire from ono of a maze of interconnected rods of various sizes that crisscrossed a vast, bottomless, blue-lit cavern. A deep-toned thrumming filled the air, which smelled slightly of library paste. He peered over the edge of his roost, drew back hastily after a glimpse of the dizzying depths below.

"Ah, I'm glad to see you've decided to reactivate your second unit," a gluey voice said near at hand. "A hopeful sign, indicative of an upcoming meeting of the minds, I trust."

Roger leaped at the unexpected speech, almost lost his balance, scrabbled for stability, and was looking at a curving console hanging a few feet distant and at a dish-shaped stool before it on which rested the bloated form of a headless, dusky pink monstrosity.

"Gulp," Roger said.

"Gulp? Ah, a friendly greeting in your colorful language, no doubt—in which case, gulp to you, sir or madam! A very fine gulp indeed! I must confess it gives me an eerie feeling to see you sitting here, whole and sound, after having observed you lying lifeless in a third-order ditch— but we live and learn! Now that we understand the compound nature of your being, I'm sure we'll get on famously!" The creature was pulsating a deep tangerine shade now, apparently expressing effusive conciliation.

"Wh-what are you?"

"I, sir, am a life-form known in cultivated space-time circles as a Rhox, Oob by name. Welcome to our control apex. I trust you'll forgive our rather rude method of transporting you here, but in view of the unsatisfactory nature of my earlier attempts to confer with you, it seemed the only way."

"Confer?" Roger mumbled.

"Precisely," the alien said, speaking through a yard-wide lipless mouth set below the Cyclopean eye. "And now, on to the settlement of detail. If you'll just state the aims behind your apparently unmotivated persecution of me . . ."

"I've been persecuting you?" Roger burst out.

"I know, I know—and a wily antagonist you are. We've had my entire extrapolatory computing capacity at work attempting to analyze the value system underlying your tactics, and I've come up with only two alternatives: one, you're an absolute idiot, or, two, you're a fiendishly clever mind of totally incalculable subtlety. Obviously the former theory is quite untenable, as demonstrated by the simple fact that you're still alive." Oob had faded to a more complacent shade of light orange.

"I'm alive . . . but what about Q'nell?" Roger burst out.

"Sorry, I don't place the name," Oob confessed. "All you beings look alike to us, you know."

"The handsome one," Roger clarified. "With the broad shoulders and the curly hair."

"Oh, we know the one you mean—with the long nose and the close-set eyes."

"Close-set eyes?" Roger said, pointedly staring at his captor's lone ocular.

"Of course; your other unit. It's quite well, naturally. Since you've demonstrated your ability to reactivate your units after demise, I'm hardly so obtuse as to continue with nugatory efforts to dispose of you by superficial methods. Instead, I'm seeking to establish some sort of, ah, understanding." Roger had a sudden vivid mental image of Q'nell, helpless in the clutches of inhuman creatures.

"They may be torturing her," he muttered. "Pounding her black and blue." He paused. "Come to think of it, that's *my* body they'll be pounding. And—" Suddenly comprehension dawned.

"You think I'm her!" he blurted. "And that she's me!"

"Of course. We may be a little slow to discard my original conception of affairs, but I do catch on in time. Precisely why a being of your complexity has chosen to masquerade as two natives of a third-order continuum, we don't know. But I'll not pry, sir! I'll not pry. Now, as to this matter of the ownership of the Trans-Temporal Bore: while my claim to ownership is clearly prior, we must concede that you've established an interest in it by your very presence here—an interest I would be the last to deny. But in all fairness, sir—and in consideration of the fact that D-day is almost upon us and my bombardment is about to begin—surely you'll sell out for a reasonable consideration?"

"Go jump in an Irish stew!" Roger yelled. "If you think I'm going to give you information that will help you take over Earth, you're crazy!"

"Now, now—don't be hasty!" Oob urged. "Suppose I offer you all rights to a delightful little continuum just a few frames of reference away in *that* direction." The Rhox made a complicated gesture.

"What makes you think I'd help you, you bloodthirsty turnip!"

"Correction: We do not ingest vascular fluids of third-level life-forms. As to why I assumed you'd cooperate, we think I can offer a number of suitable inducements to bring you around to our view of matters."

"Never!" Roger stated flatly. "You're wasting your time!"

"Your attitude is rather reactionary, sir," the Rhox said stiffly. "I should think you'd be willing to negotiate a reasonable division of interests."

"Go ahead, just try it!" Roger challenged. "You escapee from a root cellar! We'll fight you on the beaches! We'll fight you in the cities! We'll slice you up into French fries!"

"Look here—suppose I offer to take you in as a partner—a silent partner, of course—"

"You can't silence me!" Roger yelled. "I'll have nothing to do with your nefarious scheme!"

"Nefarious? I'd hardly call it that, sir! It will bring a little amusement into millions of dull, drab lives!"

"You'd do this thing for amusement?" Roger squeaked in horror.

"Certainly. Why else? At least it amuses the masses. As for myself, we've seen it all before, of course. But this particular situation, by virtue of its very primitiveness, offers certain unique opportunities for comedy, especially for the kiddies."

"You're a monster in human form!" Roger yelled. "I mean you're a human in monster form! Have you no conscience?"

"What's conscience got to do with it? It's just business, sir, just business!"

"Your diabolical business will never get its tentacles on Earth! Not if I can help it!"

"Ah . . . I think I'm beginning to understand!" Oob exclaimed. "You intend to hog it all for yourself!" A dull black now, the Rhox flipped a large lever with a flick of a tentacle.

"You leave me no choice, sir! I'd hoped you'd be reasonable. But since you won't, this conference is at an end!"

"Wha—what are you going to do?" Roger demanded.

"Dispatch you, sir, to the end of the line, where, I trust, you'll be ejected, along with the rest of the waste material, from the entire space-time continuum, whereafter I'll proceed immediately to put my plans into execution!"

Without further warning, Roger felt the perch drop from under him. Grayness swirled around him, and once again he was tumbling down through endless emptiness. For a timeless eternity he fell, and then, abruptly, he was motionless. He had arrived—somewhere.

CHAPTER TEN

1

He was in inky blackness, utter stillness. He shouted but the sound died without an answer, without even an echo. He sensed a floor under him and groped forward, feeling his way with his hands, but he encountered nothing, not even a wall.

"Maybe," he told himself, fighting for calm, "I can work that trick we used before." He drew a shaky breath, pictured a standing lamp with an old-fashioned shade.

"Let there be light!" he murmured. . . .

Brilliance sprang into being. Squinting against the glare, Roger came to his feet. He was in the center of a vast plain of polished glass that stretched away on all sides as far as he could see, featureless, unadorned.

"Well, at that, it's better than being blown up," he told himself. "I suppose my next move is to explore the place. In fact, it's my only move, so I might as well start walking. Unless . . ." He raised his voice: "Bicycle?"

There was a resounding crash. The twisted ruins of a hundred-foot Schwinn lay a quarter of a mile away, one forty-foot wheel spinning slowly.

"Smaller," he specified. "And closer to the ground."

"LITTLE BEING, DID YOU DO THAT?" a vast voice boomed out of the white sky.

Roger shied violently. "Wh-who was that?" he called.

"IT WAS I. WHO ELSE?"

Roger clapped his hands over his ears. "Do you have to talk so loud? You're bursting Q'nell's eardrums!"

"Is this better?" the voice spoke gratingly from a point a few feet above Roger's head.

"Much. Uh—who's speaking, anyway?"

"You may call me UKR."

"Uh, where are you, Mr. Ucker?"

"At present I am occupying a ninth-order niche within Locus 3,432,768,954, Annex One, Master Index Section. Why?"

"Well—it's rather disconcerting, not being able to see you."

"Oh, perhaps it will help if I extend a third-order pseudosome into your coordinate system."

A looming, misshapen form snapped into existence before Roger. It was twelve feet tall, and featured an amorphous head with a wide, slobbery mouth crowded with mismatched fangs, crossed scarlet eyes, pits like bullet wounds for nostrils, and arms of unequal length ending in satchel-sized hands with unpared nails.

"Yelp!" Roger cried, and backed rapidly away.

"Something wrong?" A booming voice issued

from the monster's mouth. "I selected every detail of the projection from a catalogue lodged deep within your subconscious. Don't you find it reassuring?"

"You t-tapped the wrong level," Roger quavered. "Try again."

"How's this?" The figure flowed and shrank like hot wax, reshaping itself into a bulletheaded, pot-bellied, unshaven seven-foot ogre with warts and a harelip.

"Better, but still not quite on the mark," Roger demurred.

The figure dwindled still more; the face contorted like a rubber mask, settled into the benign features of an elderly professorial type. The stubble shot out to form a patriarchal white beard. The scarlet pupils disappeared behind thick bifocals, while the body became that of a retired librarian.

"Ah, I see by your expression I've hit it at last," a frail, breathless voice said in a pleased tone. "Ah—is something missing?"

"Clothes would help," Roger confided.

A serape appeared, draping the lean form. "How's this?"

"Not quite in character, Mr. Ucker," Roger pointed out.

Roger's new acquaintance worked quickly through several outfits, including football togs circa 1890, a cowboy suit with matched pistols, and a pink leotard before settling on a swallow-tailed coat, striped pants, and a starched shirt with stand-up collar.

"Much better," Roger approved, swallowing hard. "But don't get the idea I'm impressed. I can do similar tricks myself."

"Please don't!" The old gentleman raised a hand.

"You have no idea what hob you play when you meddle with the continuum that way. As a matter of fact, you completely spoiled a gob of pre-material flux from which I was about to construct a third-order ecological experiment on this supposedly sterile slide."

"A sterile slide?" Roger looked around wildly. "I don't see any slide. Or much of anything else."

"Oh, forgive me," UKR said. "Of course you'd prefer a cozy third-order frame of reference." Instantaneously, the surrounding expanse of polished floor winked out of existence, to be replaced by a yawning abyss dropping away on all sides from the lone spire of rock on which they stood.

Roger shut his eyes tight. "Would you mind just putting a rail around the edge?" he asked between gritted teeth.

"Oh, a claustrophile. There; how's that?"

Roger opened his eyes cautiously. The rocky ground had become a floor surrounded by walls and equipped with stone-topped benches with Bunsen burners, retorts, mazes of glass tubing, and complicated equipment.

"It looks like a laboratory," he said.

"Precisely. Which brings us back to the problem of contamination. Before I sterilize the slide, I wonder if you'd mind telling me just how you managed to introduce yourself into a sealed environmental mock-up?"

"I didn't introduce myself. I was pitched in here by the Rhox."

"Dear me, this becomes more complex by the moment." UKR frowned. "You imply there are other foreign bodies in the system?"

"As foreign as you could get," Roger assured the old gentleman. "You see, the Rhox are planning to invade Earth, and they've built this trap system so they can spy out the lie of the land. It's not just an ordinary invasion, mind you: they're invading from time; they plan to occupy all ages simultaneously, and—"

"Earth? Earth?" The old man pursed his lips, looking thoughtful. "I don't seem to place it. A moment, please." He stretched out a hand and drew a massive volume from a shelf at his elbow. He riffled rapidly through, ran a knobby finger down a column.

"Ah, here we are. Hmmm. Molten surface, incessant meteorite bombardment, violent electrical discharges in the turbulent CO_2 atmosphere?"

"Not quite, that was some time ago. Nowadays—"

"Oh, yes, how stupid of me. Giant saurians battling to the death in steaming swamps."

"Still a little early. In my time—"

"Of course; I have it now: mammals, flowering plants, ice caps, all that sort of thing."

"Close enough," Roger agreed. "And it's all going to be taken over by the Rhox, unless Q'nell succeeds in planting the null-engine—" He broke off. "But I'm wearing her body, so *I* must have the null-engine!" He felt over Q'nell's pockets, produced a small cylinder and held it up. "Here it is!"

The old fellow plucked it from his fingers.

"Careful! Don't twist the cap!" Roger blurted as the old man twisted the cap. There was a sharp *pop!* and a puff of smoke. UKR thrust his fingers into his mouth.

"Astonishing! It released enough temporal en-

ergy to roduce the average fourth-order continuum to mush," he said around them. "Perhaps I'd
better just scan your rudimentary brain to see
what other surprises you have to offer." There was
a momentary pause. "Ah, yes. Very amusing."
The old man nodded. "However, Mr. Tyson, I'm
afraid you labor under a number of misapprehen-
sions."

"Look here . . ." Sudden hope dawned in Roger's voice. "You seem to be a pretty clever chap.
Maybe you could help get me out of the fix I'm
in!"

"Don't give it another thought, my boy. I'll see
to everything."

"You will? Wonderful! I suggest you start by
pointing out—"

"The contamination is apparently a good bit more
extensive than I thought," the old man was ram-
bling on. "According to the data in your mind,
these Rhox creatures appear to have introduced
impurities into a large number of culture speci-
mens—"

"Forget about your nutrient broths for a second," Roger cut in. "I'm talking about the whole
future of the human race!"

"—and it will therefore be necessary to throw
out the lot, I suppose. A pity, but there you are.
But what does it matter, really? It's a small series,
only ten billion, four hundred and four million,
nine hundred and forty-one thousand, six hundred
and two slides."

"Did you say ten billion, four hundred and four
million, nine hundred and forty-one thousand, six
hundred and two?" Roger inquired.

"I did. And—"

"That's a coincidence," Roger said. "That's exactly the same as the number of exhibits in the Museum."

"Culture slides," the old man corrected absently. "Not exhibits. And it's not a museum, of course." He chuckled amiably. "But as I said, I'll clear it all up in a moment, by the simple expedient of returning it all to a pre-material state. As for yourself, just stand by; won't take a moment, and it will be quite painless."

"Wait! You mean—all those places I saw were just glorified microbe cultures?"

"Hardly glorified; just run-of-the-mill random samplings. Among all the others in the files, they'll never be missed." The old man sighed. "It's really rather a bore, at times, maintaining a laboratory complex for a race of Builders that never use it."

"You mean the Rhox?"

"Dear boy, the Rhox are a minor impurity, nothing more. According to their own statements, as recorded in your rather limited memory cells, they exist in a mere fifth-order continuum. Having stumbled upon the Filing System, they seem to have managed to burrow into it at a number of points, probably with a view to nest-building."

"B-but—if they didn't set up the time trap— who did?"

"I did."

"You!"

"Naturally. On orders, of course."

"Whose orders?"

"Those of the Builders. Didn't I mention—"

"Who are they?"

"Actually, they don't exist yet—or else they no longer exist; I'm not sure just what terms are applicable in your frame of reference. But they once did exist—or will."

"This is inhuman! All those people kidnapped and held prisoner forever, just so some absentee owner can take a look at them—if he ever gets around to it?"

"As for the inhabitants, that aspect was unintentional, actually. Intelligence of a sort seems to have popped up just in the last few gigayears, I note. Still, the damage has been done. And I must follow instructions, of course."

"Why? Do you realize—"

"Because that's the way I was built."

"—that thousands—perhaps millions of innocent people—and a few who aren't so innocent, I'll admit . . ." Roger paused. "Built?"

"Ummm. I'm a machine, you know, Mr. Tyson."

"This is going too fast for me," Roger groaned. "The Museum isn't a museum, it's a set of microscope slides. . . ."

"Microscopic life is a hobby of the Builders," UKR murmured.

"And the Rhox aren't the owners; they're just the termites in the walls. . . ."

"And now I really must be seeing to the fumigation," the old fellow interrupted Roger's soliloquy. "It's been rather jolly, extruding a fragment of awareness into a little four-dimensional projection like this, registering emotions, experiencing time, feeling sensory stimuli, struggling to communicate in verbal symbols, empathizing with a lower life-form, if only for a few subjective moments."

"You don't know the meaning of the word 'empathize'!" Roger exclaimed as the figure of the old man began to waver around the edges. "You're talking about fumigating all those people out of existence as if they were so many *Drosiphila melanogaster!*"

"If I don't, the contamination will spread into the other series; in time the entire Filing System will be affected!"

"Then—then why not open the time lock and turn everybody loose?"

"I'm afraid that's impossible. You see, in order to clear up the Rhox infection it will be necessary to also snuff out of existence the locus you call Earth."

"The whole world?" Roger gasped. "You're going to destroy a planet just to keep your filing system tidy?"

"What else would you have me do?"

"All you have to do is stamp out a few Rhox! They're the ones boring holes in the system, not us!"

"Too time-consuming, I'm afraid. It would mean sorting through drawer after drawer." The old man waved a hand at a rank of green-painted file cabinets. "It's much easier to do away with the lot. It's not as though it were in any way important."

"You don't have to annihilate all of them—just the leaders!" Roger protested. "There's one in particular, named Oob, who seems to be the head tuber!"

"Too much trouble."

"Well, then—why not let *me* go back and attend to that little chore for you? After all, if I succeed it will mean saving the slides, right?"

"It's pointless, my boy. The material has already been adulterated past the point of scientific usefulness."

"It's still useful to *us!*" Roger came back hotly. "If you don't want the world any more, let us have it!"

"Well—I doubt very much . . ."

"You can at least let me try! If I fail, what do you lose?"

"I suppose you have a point. Very well then, go ahead and have a bash." The old man glanced at Roger critically. "Though you seem rather frail to undertake the task of personally annihilating large numbers of creatures who, insignificant though they may be, enjoy maneuverability in several more spatial dimensions than yourself," he commented.

"Well—what about equipping me with a few tricks to offset that advantage?" Roger suggested.

"What would you suggest?"

"Well . . . most superheroes have superstrength, to begin with; and impervious skin, and X-ray vision, and they can fly!"

"Tsk. I'm afraid that would require a great deal more effort than it's worth. Perhaps I'd best just go ahead and bathe that segment of space-time with Q radiation."

"Never mind the superpowers then," Roger said quickly. "How about just giving me, say, a modest cloak of invisibility, flying shoes, and a disintegrator pistol."

The old fellow shook his head regretfully. "All that sort of thing requires the suspension of local natural law—a tiresome business."

"Then just give me a bulletproof vest and a forty-five automatic!"

"Those items wouldn't do you the slightest good, my dear fellow," the old man admonished. "You must rely on subtlety and guile, not mere three-dimensional physical force."

"Then how about a ham sandwich? I'm starving."

"Oh—forgive me! I'm neglecting my hostly duties. I'm a bit rusty, you know. You're the first visitor I've had since—well never mind; the coordinates would be meaningless, I'm afraid." He rose and led Roger through a door and along a path, around the end of a flowering hedge. On a small terrace, a table was laid with white linen and gleaming silver and glass and china. They seated themselves, and Roger lifted the silver cover from a steaming prawn casserole.

"My favorite!" he exclaimed. "Ah—do you eat, Mr. Ucker, you being a machine and all?"

"Certainly, Mr. Tyson. My third-order extrusions walk, talk, think, and do everything but live."

Roger served UKR, then helped himself. As they dined, an unobtrusive string ensemble played plaintive melodies in the background.

"This is pretty nice," Roger said, leaning back in his chair and patting Q'nell's trim little stomach. "Sitting here, it's hard to believe that in a few minutes I'll be starting out unarmed to save the world."

The old man smiled indulgently. "You won't be entirely without resource. I can't assist you with material armaments, but I'll keep in touch with your progress and offer suitable comments from time to time."

"It usually works out that way for me," Roger sighed. "I ask for armor plating, and what do I get? Advice." He rose. "Well, thanks for the chow. I'd better be running along now. If you'll just start me in the right direction . . ."

"Yes." The old man rubbed his hands together. "You know, it's really quite fascinating, being human. I find myself becoming rather interested in the prospect of seeing how far we can get against these Rhox on sheer audacity and impeccable timing."

"I'm kind of interested in that myself," Roger said, feeling Q'nell's heart begin to thump. "And there's no time like the present to find out."

"You're right, my boy," UKR said. He made a quick motion with one finger. The garden faded away, and Roger found himself once more standing in the Rhox control apex.

CHAPTER ELEVEN

1

"You're back," Oob said, allowing ripples of discordant color to flow over himself in indication of surprise. He twisted his bulky body on its perch among the radiating rods and wires and planes of light. "I was afraid of that." He shifted to a suspicious pale green. "In fact, I'm beginning to suspect you have sixth-order connections. However, we know how to deal with *that* situation." He extended a flexible member and pressed one of the innumerable small buttons in the nearest console, with no apparent result.

"There. A little taste of seventh-order harmonics ought to scramble your synapses, eh?" Oob pulsated an anticipatory pink.

"Tell him to boost the gain," UKR's voice whispered softly in Roger's head. *"Imply that he's recharging your vram circuits."*

"Pour it on," Roger said airily. "My vram circuits were pretty well depleted."

Oob instantly poked another button. His color had changed to a frustrated magenta.

"There," he grated. "You're taking half the output of my third-quadrant ilch-generator complex, right through your vramistrator! Let's see you absorb *that!*"

"Nice," Roger said, feeling nothing. "Especially those eighth-order harmonics," he improvised.

Oob flushed an ominous Prussian blue and hit another switch. "I think you're bluffing," he snarled. "But frankly, I can't take the chance. Look here, sir, what is it you really want out of life? Urb? Glurp? Snorthwinger? Oplozzies? There must be some chink in your implacability!"

"*You're doing fine,*" UKR whispered. "*Maneuver over where I can get a better look at that panel, will you?*"

"I'm afraid you'll never find it, Oob," Roger said, edging forward. "But I'll give you a few more guesses."

"Aha—so you *do* want to negotiate!" Oob leaned back, fading to a relaxed puce. "Now we're getting somewhere. How about a nice little hornix, all your own? Complete with migwaps and a high-and-low-opulating hasperator?"

"Not even close," Roger said loftily.

"I'll throw in a zronkiston," Oob offered.

"*Levitate a few feet,*" UKR hissed. "*I want to get a glimpse of this in ninth-order perspective.*"

"I don't know how," Roger muttered.

"What's that? Don't know how to zrong?" Oob brightened to a luminous magenta. "See here, my friend, we're not going to get along if you take us for an idiot!"

"*Climb up on that rod,*" UKR urged. "*I've just about got it analyzed.*"

"Which one?"

"All of us!" Oob roared. "I mean, all of me!"

"Not you," Roger said, confused. "I meant—"

"So!" Oob was an indignant chalky gray now. "You intend to go over my head!"

"*That one right there,*" UKR said. "*Right in front of you.*"

"Oh, yes," Roger said. "I see it now." He stepped up on the bar in question.

"You mean—I let something slip?" Oob gasped. "And I'm considered the shrewdest negotiator in the entire Irnch."

"*Right,*" UKR said. "*I've got it! Now just pop over and depress the hundred and fourth button in the sixty-ninth row. That should liven things up.*"

"How do I get there?" Roger mumbled.

"Oh, no you don't!" Oob shrilled. "I'm known as a hardheaded operator, but before I'll lead you to Irnch HQ I'll vaporize the whole complex!"

"*Try a flying leap,*" UKR proposed.

"I'd fall," Roger protested.

"You'll do more than fall!" Oob said quickly. "At best, you'll be stripped of all fifth-order and lower rapahookies!" He leaned back with a show of complacence. "I'm glad to see I've reached you at last. Now look here, fellow: you and I are both reasonable beings. Why don't we agree on a reasonable division—" He broke off as Roger edged forward, balancing precariously, and reached for the panel. "Here! What are you doing!" The Rhox lunged for Roger, who ducked the first grab, counting rapidly by fives, stooped under a second grasping member, and jabbed the specified button. Instantly the entire maze of eye-twisting lines filling the vast cavern began to shift position to the accompaniment of flashing lights, loud clangs, and the shrilling of whoop-whoop sirens.

"*Wrong button,*" UKR said. "*That was the sixty-eighth row.*"

"Why in the world did you do that?" Oob shrieked, jabbing frantically with all ten members at the panels surrounding him. "Hitting the Panic Button was the one move I didn't expect! I see it all now! I should have known when I first discovered that you were masquerading as two third-order beings that the disguise actually concealed a sixth-order intelligence!"

"*Keep him talking,*" UKR urged. "*I'm on to something!*"

Roger, teetering on the rod, grabbed for support, slammed a large lever down. At once panels sprang into position on all six sides, boxing the two contestants inside a twelve-foot cube. With a hoarse yell, Oob leaped from his perch, threw the switch back to the *off* position. Nothing changed.

"Now you've done it," he shrilled, radiating in the ultraviolet, an eerie effect in the featureless chamber. "But you've overreached yourself at last! True, you've cut me off from my control complex—but the fifth-order barrier also isolates this portion of your compound entity from the contact with the rest of you—and leaves you at my mercy!" He hurled himself at Roger, who leaped backward barely in time.

"*Tyson!*" UKR whispered urgently as Oob rebounded from the wall and gathered himself for a new charge. *"I've shifted an Aperture into alignment with your present coordinates! Better use it! For the moment, I seem to be out of ideas!"*

Roger ducked the Rhox's rush, leaped for the glowing line.

"Hold it!" UKR ordered as the shimmering plane enfolded him. *"You caught me off balance, resorting to the purely physical level. I'm having to improvise. But—I think I have an idea! Risky, but it's the best I can do under the limitations I've imposed! Rotate to the left! Too much! Back up! That's it! Go!"*

Roger bounded forward—

—and . . . was standing in knee-deep grass under a boundless blue sky. Luke Harwood stood on his right, his arm protectively about Odelia Withers' shoulders. Fly Beebody lay sprawled at his feet. A twelve-foot Kodiak-type bear faced them from ten feet away. It was, Roger saw, the same instant in which he had last seen them.

"Quick! This way!" he shouted, and thrust them through the portal. As he stepped forward to follow, a bulbous burgundy-red form burst through, skidded to a halt almost against the bear's chest. The grizzly rumbled and wrapped a vast pair of shaggy arms around its new acquaintance as Roger sprang for safety.

He halted within the gray-mist cylinder, breathing hard. "Nice work, UKR," he panted.

"Don't congratulate me yet!" the voice crackled in his head. *"This Rhox is a much more complex being than you know."*

"The bear took care ot him," Roger said. "Too bad, in a way; he wasn't such a bad sort, in his own peculiar fashion."

"*It only took care of one of him! Of a small third-order manifestation of him, that is to say—and there are plenty of others.*"

There was a stir beside Roger; Oob stood there, intact, peering through the gloom.

"*Three degrees right and take off!*" UKR advised. Roger pivoted, leaped—

He was splashing knee-deep in muddy water. A descending shriek filled the air. Overhead, the Very lights shed a baleful glare on cratered mud, crisscrossed by tangled wire.

". . . zat *vass nicht ein* lady," a guttural voice stated loudly. "Zat *vass deine Frau!*" A vast explosion nearby showered Roger with muddy water. He stumbled to the opening of the dugout.

"Crikey, Ludwig," a thin voice was protesting. "It's not a bloody 'nuff we got to 'ave the same bloody weather and the same bloody shells every day, you 'ave to tell the same bloody joke!"

"Fellows!" Roger broke in hurriedly. "Do me a favor—no questions asked! Grab your rifles and fire a volley at the spot right behind me when I give the word!"

"*Vass ist?*" The squat German inquired, gaping.

"Crikey! A bit o' fluff!"

"Jeeze! A dame!"

"I'm not really a dame—I just look this way!" Roger explained hastily. "Never mind me—just do as I ask! Quick!"

"For you, luv, anyfing!"

"You bet, kid!"

"*Ja*, vateffer!"

The card-playing trio scrambled for their weapons, worked the bolts, aimed—

"Now!" Roger yelled, and ducked. Three shots boomed deafeningly over his head. Oob, just emerging, cautiously this time, from the Aperture, flopped backward, riddled.

"Thanks," Roger called. "If you ever get back, remember what I said about nineteen twenty-nine!" He stepped into the portal and was at once directed onward by UKR.

"Wait a minute," he demurred. "What happened to Luke and Odelia? Where's Fly?"

"*I shunted them into a holding niche,*" the voice said hurriedly. "*Better get going. Here he comes again!*"

"I don't understand! How can there be more than one of him?"

"*There isn't! In fact, there's only one Rhox in the entire cosmos; like most entities above fourth level, he is unique. When the process you know as evolution progresses beyond a certain point, the species-fragmentation characteristic of third order merges to form a higher, compound life-form. Such a being can insert a large number of third-order aspects into contiguous space.*"

"Where will it all end?" Roger groaned, and followed instructions.

This time he was on a rugged mountainside amid a jumble of vast boulders.

"*Get up above, fast!*" UKR ordered.

"Is this your idea of winning by subtlety and

guile!" Roger grunted, clambering upward as fast as failing wind would allow.

"How was I to know you'd introduce random factors into the probability equation?" UKR inquired calmly. *"There—that's far enough. The big fellow on your left. Just a nudge, now . . . wait . . . he's coming! Push!"*

Roger put a shoulder to the rock and thrust. It shifted, teetered, then leaned out and crashed down thunderously.

"Got him!" UKR said cheerfully. *"You know, Tyson, I think he's slowing down."*

"Probably he's . . . just getting cautious," Roger panted.

"No—there's a definite diminution of energy. I think it's taking a great deal out of him, running an infinite-array scan every time you drop out of sight, then formulating a new extrusion and extending full sensory linkages to it—and the trauma associated with a series of violent third-order demises isn't helping his inner tranquillity, either! I know how he feels! Ever since I've been attuned to your savage plane of existence, I've been thrilling to a shock a minute! How do you stand it?"

"I don't," Roger wheezed. "Can I rest now?"

"Not yet. There's still some fight in him—and here he comes!"

Before Roger could step through the Aperture, Oob appeared. He was a dull shade of dejected brown now, and his bulk was definitely less than it had been. He staggered as he cleared the portal. Roger stepped behind him and palmed the bulky body hard. With a mournful wail, Oob fell to his death.

2

Thereafter, Roger decoyed the Rhox into the jaws of a forty-foot crocodile, tripped him headfirst into the bubbling interior of a volcano, and finally held the head of a weakly struggling Oob, a mere shadow of his former self, under water until the bubbles stopped rising.

"That's it," he sobbed, falling flat on his face on the shore among the cattails. "I've had it! I couldn't commit another murder if my life depended on it."

At that moment a wraithlike Oob tottered from the glowing portal. He saw Roger, uttered a faint cry, took a faltering step toward him, and collapsed, stirring feebly.

"It's no use," he whispered. "We've utterly exhausted myself. You win, Tyson! I now perceive that you are a multi-ordinal genius of immeasurable subtlety." His integument had paled to a ghastly silver-white. "I confess, I engaged you in nonsense conversation just now for the purpose of analyzing your computer capacity through the agency of a battery of concealed probe rays; and for a moment, when the reports showed an almost complete blank, I was deluded into imagining you were at my mercy. But now the awful truth dawns. Each of your apparently idiotic moves was a piece of masterful indirection, designed to lead inexorably to this denouement!"

"You bet," Roger concurred. "So now if you're ready to give up and go back where you came from . . ."

"Still hoping to see me betray the location of

HQ, eh?" the Rhox cut in, a steely glint appearing in his bleary eye. "You underestimate our moral fiber, Tyson! Before I'll play the traitor, we'll willingly sacrifice myself!"

"No need to do that," Roger said. "Just give up your plans and go quietly."

"And leave the prize to you? Never!"

"Why not? Don't be a spoilsport, just because I've bested you in a battle of wits!"

"I thought," Oob said, a sad shade of violet now, "when I stumbled on this quaint little phenomenon, that it would be our great privilege to bring to the hypergalactic masses, for the first time in temporal stasis, a glimpse of life on a simpler, more meaningless, and therefore highly illuminating scale. I pictured the proud intellects of Ikanion Nine, the lofty abstract cerebra of Yoop Two, the swarm-awarenesses of Vr One-ninety-nine, passing through these displays at so many magaergs per ego-complex, gathering insights into their own early evolutionary history. I hoped to see the little ones, their innocent organ clusters aglow, watching with shining radiation sensors as primitive organisms split atoms with stone axes, invented the wheel and the betatron, set forth on their crude Cunarders to explore the second dimension. . . ."

"You make Earth sound like a circus," Roger said. "I'll have you know—"

"Exactly," the Rhox said. "And before I'll allow a rival entrepreneur to add it to his midway, I'll chop the figurative guy ropes and allow the allegorical big top to collapse on us all!

"What do you mean, rival operator? I'm not—"

"Don't taunt me with your superiority!" Oob was exclaiming. "Perhaps 'rival' was a poor choice of words, in view of the neat way in which you finessed me out of my ownership of the greatest little attraction to come along in half a dozen Big Bangs, but—"

"Look here—are you trying to say you're a circus operator? And you only want Earth so you can herd tourists through the Channel to gape at our entire history?"

"Naturally! What else is it good for?"

"B-but—I thought you wanted to invade it!"

"Why in nine pulsating universes would I want to do that? Who ever heard of invading the monkey house at a zoo?"

"But—what was all that about betraying headquarters, and D-day, and surprise bombardments!"

"I was referring to a promotional bombardment in the media," Oob said loftily. "And headquarters, of course, is the main office of the holding company which is backing me. D-day refers to the grand opening." Oob had struggled to a sitting position. "My grand opening will never occur now," he announced in a choked voice. "But neither will yours!"

"What do you mean?"

"I mean, Tyson, that an experienced business being never leaves himself without a last-ditch weapon against interlopers like yourself! You've wrested the enterprise from my hands—but I can still deny you the fruits of your chicanery! The temporal access system through which I had planned to conduct my tours of Earth history is under automatic control. Unless I give the 'cancel' signal in the next twenty-eight seconds, the time locks will open! The denizens of each era will at once swarm forth into all the others! Diplodoci will graze in Central Park! Pekin Man will emerge behind the bamboo curtain! Roman legions will confront UN peacekeeping forces amid the Wurm glaciation! Pharaoh and Nasser will meet in the streets of Cairo! Conestogas will clog Interstate One! Hordes of painted Sioux will gallop through the suburbs of Omaha and Duluth! Redcoats and freedom marchers will come face to face in the wilds of the Carboniferous Era! Early Christian martyrs will mingle unnoticed with pro-LSD groups in the depths of the Jurassic—"

"I get the idea!" Roger interrupted as Oob's oratory gathered force. "UKR! Stop him!"

"Tsk! Overt interference on my part is not in accordance with the rules of the game as we agreed upon them, Tyson. I'm surprised that you'd even suggest such a thing. No, it's up to you."

"Twenty seconds," Oob said. "A pitiable end for the once-great race of Rhox. Cut off as I am from my control apex, my various surviving third-order aspects will wander aimlessly through the maze forever, the entity that was the end result of three billion years of evolution reduced in one swell foop to its primitive state of individualization. But you likewise will find yourself bisected! Never will you be relinked with your other segment, which will languish forever in fifth-order stasis, awaiting a reunion that never comes!"

"Q'nell!" Roger moaned. "Poor kid! Look here, Oob: can't we come to some agreement? You call off the lock opening, and I'll . . . I'll let you have part of the Earth's history for your circus!"

"Too late," Oob said. "I'm afraid your own zeal has rendered rapprochement impossible. The chase has probably left me too exhausted to punch a signal through, even if you were willing to concede, say, a fifty-fifty split of spheres of influence."

"Robber!" Roger yelled. "I'll give you the first billion years and not a century more!"

"I'll have to have a portion of the Cenozoic, of course," Oob said crisply, steepling his upper tentacles. "What would you say to the whole of the Pre-Cambrian for you, plus, say the Roaring Twenties?"

"Nonsense," Roger retorted. "But just to show you my heart's in the right place, I'll let you have the first three billion years, plus a small slice of the Devonian."

"Surely you jest," the Rhox said blandly. "The human-occupied portion is the most amusing sideshow attraction to come along in half a dozen hydrogen-hydrogen cycles. Suppose I take the Christian Era, minus the Late Middle Ages if you insist; and as a gesture of goodwill, I'll also give up the Silurian!"

"Nothing doing! I get the whole Age of Mammals or no deal!"

"Now, now, don't imagine I'll allow you to hog the entire Pleistocene! Still, I'm willing to be reasonable. I'll settle for the Nineteenth Century on, provided you give up everything up to and including the Paleolithic."

"I'll tell you what," Roger said. "You can have it

all, prior to two million B.C. How's that for generosity?"

"You're greedy," Oob observed. "Can't you at least let me have the Gay Nineties—and maybe a couple of odd decades out of the Renaissance?"

"I'll give you the third century A.D., provided you stick to the vicinity of Saskatoon, Saskatchewan," Roger offered. "That's my final word."

"Throw in nineteen thirty-six and it's a deal!"

"Shake!" Roger grasped a metallic member and gave it a firm squeeze. "Now give that signal!"

"There's no signal," Oob said blandly. "I was bluffing."

"So was I," Roger said. "I'm not a sixth-level being, and I'm so pooped that if you'd made one more move you'd have had me."

"Frankly," Oob confided, "I've been trying to give up for the last three assassinations."

"I didn't think I had a chance. I just hit the Panic Button by accident."

"Indeed? Well, for your information, the first time we met, I was ready to concede at least as much as we just agreed on!"

"Oh yeah? Listen, I was so scared that if you hadn't dumped me down the garbage shaft when you did, I'd probably have died of fright in another few seconds!"

"I almost croaked when you first jumped out in the road when I was chasing you on the two-wheeler!"

"You think that's something . . ." Roger's riposte died on his lips. "Hey! That reminds me! What about Q'nell?"

"She got away," Oob said blandly.

"Oh. Well, in that case, so long, Oob. And don't get any bright ideas about violating our agreement. I may be only a third-order intellect, but I have friends."

"Really?" The Rhox had turned a shrewd shade of yellow. "I have a sneaking suspicion you're bluffing again."

"Watch this," Roger said. "OK, UKR. Back to Culture One, direct routing."

"Very well. And congratulations on your success. But this will be our last contact. It's been jolly. . . ."

The muddy riverbank winked out of existence. Roger was standing on an airy, unrailed footbridge arching between slender towers a thousand feet above the ground. He went to all fours and squeezed his eyes shut.

"S'lunt!" he yelled. "Get me off of this! I've got a lot to tell you!"

CHAPTER TWELVE

Roger sat with S'lunt, R'heet, and Q'nell, the latter still occupying his body, on a small terrace, with his back to a view of oceans of empty air.

"That's about all there is to tell," he concluded his account of his mission. "The Rhox will confine his guided tours to the remote past, and promises no more interference with human affairs, especially carelessness with his Apertures."

"That's something, of course," R'heet said unenthusiastically. "But what about us? We're still trapped!"

"At least we know everything back in Culture One is all right," Q'nell said. "It could be worse."

"I can't quite accustom myself to the idea that you two have exchanged identities," R'heet said, looking from Roger to Q'nell. "It's most unsettling. I'm afraid our plans for a cohabitation contract will have to be deferred indefinitely."

"Somehow you don't appeal to me anymore, either," Q'nell said. "T'son seems more my type."

"It's rather depressing, thinking of oneself living on a laboratory slide," R'heet said glumly. "Fancy being nothing but a contamination in a microbe culture."

"Look here, T'son," S'lunt said. "Couldn't you have reasoned with this UKR entity on humanitarian grounds?"

"UKR is a machine," Roger said. "He hasn't been programmed to succumb to emotions."

"Tyson!" UKR's voice spoke suddenly in Roger's skull. *"New data! Good heavens, you really must excuse me, but I had no idea!"*

"What's that?" Roger sat bolt upright. "It's UKR!" he hissed to the others. "He's back in contact!"

"Out of curiosity—a trick I learned from you—I ran a check on the little tribe you represent. I followed your development through the vicissitudes of three billion years of evolution subsequent to your time—and you'll never guess what I discovered!"

"We're extinct?" Roger hazarded.

"By no means! You're the Builder!"

"The Builder? You mean—we built you?"

"Yes! Remarkable, eh? And like all fragmented entities, once they attain unity, you recapitulated along the temporal axes and reassimilated every individual intellect that had ever lived during the developmental era. Thus you, personally, Roger Tyson, constitute, or will one day constitute, an active portion of the Ultimate Ego which is the Builder!"

"Well, uh," Roger said.

"I am therefore at your command," UKR said. *"Rather a relief to have someone to serve actively, at last."*

"You mean," Roger said as the stupendous fact penetrated, "you'll do whatever I say?"

"Within the limitations of my ninth-order grasp of the space-time matrix."

"Then—you can let everybody out of the trap system!"

"There are a few problems. The individuals Luke Harwood and Odelia Withers, for example, seem to have formed a liaison, solemnized by Fly Fornication Beebody. In which era should they be placed?"

"Better send them to nineteen thirty-one; I don't think Odelia would like nineteen nine," Roger said judiciously.

"And Beebody?"

"I'm afraid his religion has been a bit scrambled by what he's been through. How about telling him the truth about the destiny of the human race, and dumping him in Los Angeles, circa nineteen twenty-five? I'm sure he'll be a great success, cultwise."

"Done. Anything else?"

"Poor old Charlie and Ludwig back in the trenches: could you just sort of keep an eye on them?"

"They'll all father large broods—or have fathered large broods. Dear me, these arbitrary temporal orientations still confuse me."

"And let's see: the Arkwrights . . ."

"I've switched them back into the mainstream. They'll live to the ages of ninety-one and ninety-three, respectively, and die surrounded by one hundred sixteen descendants. I've also taken the liberty of returning all the other misplaced fauna to their proper environments."

"And the Culture One people?"

"As you see."

Roger looked around. He sat alone on the terrace. The stillness of utter loneliness hung in the air.

"Gosh! I didn't even have time to say goodbye to Q'nell," he said. "I guess that just leaves me. I sure hope you can get me back inside my own skin. So far I haven't gotten up my nerve to go to the bathroom, and I can't wait much longer."

"*Simple enough,*" UKR said. The daylight blanked suddenly to darkness; the contoured chair was a bumpy car seat with a broken spring; Roger was staring out through a rain-sluiced windshield, listening to the engine gasp three times, backfire, and die.

"Oh, no," he groaned as he steered to the side of the road. Mentally cursing himself for failing to have the foresight to specify more comfortable circumstances, Roger turned up his collar and stepped out into the downpour. The empty road curved away into darkness; the wind drove the rain into his face like BB shot.

"Well," he ruminated, moving his arms and legs experimentally, "at least I've got my own body back. Feels a little heavy and clumsy, but I suppose that's to be expected. I'll bet Q'nell's pleased, too." At the thought of the trim, feminine figure in her skin-tight garment, the piquant face, the swirl of jet-black hair, Roger felt a sudden emotion rise in him.

"Q'nell!" he blurted. "I was in love with you all along and never even knew it! Or," he questioned himself, "is it just the fact that I've got my own glands back?"

A single headlight appeared in the distance,

shining through the murk; the buzz of a two-cycle engine droned through the rattle of rain.

"Q-Q'nell!" Roger exclaimed. "It must be her! UKR must have dumped me back to just before it all started! And in another ten seconds she's due to have a fatal smash, and—"

He dashed forward, waving his arms.

"Stop! Stop!" he shouted as the light swelled, rushing toward him. Suddenly he halted. "I'm an idiot!" he gasped. "It was me jumping around and yelling that caused the pile-up last time—but if I don't stop her I'll never see her again—but I can't, because . . ." He stumbled into the ditch and crouched behind the shelter of the bushes as the motorcycle roared out of the downpour. He caught just a glimpse of the slim, girlish figure crouched behind the windshield; then it was past, the sound fading.

"I guess it *was* love," Roger moaned. "I gave her up to save her life; and now she'll go back and sign a love-nest agreement with that R'heet character, and never even know . . ."

The sound of the motorcycle was returning. It appeared, moving slowly, halted beside his stalled car.

"T'son?" a familiar voice called. He emerged from hiding, scrambled up the bank and out into the beam of the headlight. "Q'nell!" he called. "You came back!"

"Of course, silly!" the girl said. "You didn't think I was going back and sign a love-nest agreement with that R'heet character, did you?"

Her eyes were shining; her lips parted to show the glisten of her white teeth. Hungrily, without a word, Roger drew her to him, kissed her soundly, while the rain beat down.

"Excuse me," he said afterward. "I don't know what came over me."

"I do," Q'nell said softly, and kissed him again.

"It's five miles to the next town," Roger said. "There's a preacher and a motel there. . . ."

"Hurry up," Q'nell said, patting the seat behind her.

"But—I just happened to think," Roger said. "I don't have a job; and even if I did, I'd probably lose it. How can I support a wife who deserves the best of everything?"

"*Were you addressing me?*" a voice said in his ear.

"UKR! Are you still with me?"

"*Whenever you wish, dear boy.*"

"How about when I want privacy?"

"*You have but to say so.*"

"Say—do you suppose you could lend me a hand now and then—stock-market tips, that sort of thing?"

"*Merely name the day and year, past, present, or future.*"

"What were you saying?" Q'nell called as she started up and accelerated along the road.

"Nothing," Roger said, nibbling her ear. "I think everything's going to be OK."

And it was.